TEMPTING THE FOOTMAN

The House of Devon Book 5

LAUREN SMITH

Copyright 2020 by Lauren Smith
Cover Art by Jaycee DeLorenzo

ISBN: 978-1-952063-06-0 (e-book edition)
ISBN: 978-1-952063-07-7 (print edition)

❧ I ❧

LONDON · OCTOBER 1818

"What you need, my dear, is a trip to the country."

Venetia Dunham lay stretched out on a chaise, a Gothic novel abandoned in her lap as she stared up at the intricate crown molding of the ceiling in her Mayfair townhouse. She lowered her gaze to the speaker, her grandmother, Gwendolyn Dunham, the Dowager Countess of Latham.

She was *Gran* to Venetia, but *Gwen* or *Lady Latham* to everyone else. The old woman looked frail only because of her delicate bones and the walking cane she was never without. But anyone with even a passing relationship with the dowager countess knew that those bones encased a sharp tongue and an even sharper wit, and the cane was more of a weapon than a crutch, as many young men of the *ton* would attest to.

She was Venetia's constant companion, the salve to her aching heart when her mother died, and her delightful mentor and dear friend in the eleven years since. Though they were of different generations, Venetia and her gran had a bond that could not be shaken.

"I mean it, Venetia. It has been a year since Andrew passed. We're both out of mourning, and we need to escape that buffoon who has claimed his title. There are only so many things one can bear, and poor company is by far the worst." Gwen sat with her back straight, her mouth twisted in a slight scowl. Her words held a cutting edge that bore a mix of impa-tience and sadness at the dreadful situation they found themselves in.

Venetia smiled a little at Gran's reference to her cousin, Patrick, who had become the new Earl of Latham. When Venetia's father had passed suddenly, she and Gran had become the unexpected guests to her late uncle's son as he took over their townhouse as the new owner.

Gran, who hadn't seen Patrick since he was a boy, had spent five minutes alone with him after the funeral and had declared him to be a cad. Now, a year later, Venetia and Gran were living with him and the situation was quite unbearable.

"If I have to hear any more about his plans to renovate the townhouse, I shall perish on the spot. A *cardroom* to replace the drawing room? Does the fool plan to run a gambling hell?" Gwen stamped her cane's metal tip hard into the rug.

"I think you're right, Gran," Venetia said gently. "We must go to the country, I only wish we could go to our old country house." Patrick had sold it the moment he'd had a chance. That particular sale had been most injurious to Venetia. Her father had left a vast sum of money in Venetia's possession under a trust managed by an old friend of her father's, but the townhouse and the country estate, Latham House, were firmly in Patrick's control. The loss of the money had infuriated her cousin, but he'd held his temper in check. Venetia was relieved that marriage between first cousins wasn't allowed, or else she would have been worried that Patrick would try to force a marriage simply to obtain her fortune. And marriage was the very last thing Venetia wanted.

"One does not need to own a country house to visit the country." Gwen removed a small folded letter from a pocket hidden in her skirts and waved it with a triumphant smile.

Venetia sat up and set her book aside. "What is that?"

"Our escape, my dear. It's a letter from Marrian Hampton." Gwen passed her the letter.

Venetia stared at the letter's signature; her lips parted as she scanned the contents. "The Duchess of Devon?"

"Exactly. She was a dear friend of your mother's, and she has invited us to a house party in two days. I say we accept."

"But, Gran, are you up to the rigors of a house party? You've been unwell these last few months." Venetia hadn't missed Gran's increasing reliance on her cane or the pallor of her skin. Andrew's death had been especially hard on Gwen.

Gwen waved away her granddaughter's concerns. "Pish. I'm not unwell, but it serves me to appear to be."

"But why?"

"If you must know, it's Patrick. I cannot stand him, nor do I trust him. And as I am your only trust worthy escort for public events, my absence due to ill health prevents you from spending time with him where he might drag you away to marry you to some friend of his. But I cannot always pretend to be on death's door to keep you safe. At some point, he may send me away and hire a chaperone he can bribe to be absent for the moment he finds a way to get you compromised by one of those friends."

Venetia tried not to think about Patrick stooping so low as to trick her into marrying one of his friends. "Have you truly been feigning illness?"

"Yes, for the most part. Aren't I quite the actress?" Gwen's giggle was so animated that Venetia's concerns abated slightly.

"Now, what do you say? Shall we attend this house party in the country?"

Venetia examined the letter again, seeing quite clearly the duchess's invitation. "I suppose it would be nice . . ."

Just then the drawing room door opened and Patrick strode in. He wore a finely cut waistcoat and striped pantaloons, which quite dandified him. Selling her father's country estate had lined Patrick's pockets well, and he'd made it clear to Venetia and their grandmother that he wasn't afraid to spend it.

"Ah, Venetia, there you are." Patrick smiled. "I was hoping you'd be up for a ride in Hyde Park with me. There are a few friends I would like to introduce you to, especially Mr. Bernard Kenyon. He's a dear chap, quite taken with you, and he's only glimpsed you from afar. I think you would suit each other well." The entire speech was delivered quickly, and it was quite obvious that Patrick didn't realize his motives were blindingly clear.

"Patrick, I told you—with my trust, I've no need of marriage."

Patrick's smile withered, and a cold edge glinted in his eyes.

"I know you think that will satisfy you, I'm the

head of this family now, and it is my wish that you marry."

Venetia rose slowly from the couch. Her temper, which rarely flared, had sprung to life at her cousin's threat. It seemed to her horror, Gran was right about her cousin. She'd been desperately not wishing to believe it but she could deny it no longer.

"Patrick, let us lay our cards upon the table and speak frankly. You wish for me to marry one of your friends. I have no doubt the arrangement would be that you would have been paid by this new husband from part of my money he would acquire control of after the marriage. I have the right of it, do I not?"

Red suffused Patrick's face as fury took over. "Now see here, Venetia. I have tried to be polite this past year, but my kindness is at an end." He grasped her arms quite forcefully. His grip was so tight that Venetia gasped as pain shot up her arms. He gave her a violent shake, and Venetia was so stunned that she couldn't react.

But Gwen did. In a fluid motion, she swung her cane in a rapier-like arc to land between their bodies.

"Release her, Patrick. Now." The steel in her tone clanged like a fencing blade.

Patrick seemed to recover himself and released Venetia, then took a measured step back as he straightened his waistcoat and cleared his throat.

"My apologies, cousin. That was undeserved. You hurt my feelings with your unwarranted accusations. I request again that you accompany me on a ride to meet Mr. Kenyon."

Patrick's sudden and unexpected brutality had made one thing clear to Venetia—she and her grandmother could not stay here any longer.

"I will go change into my riding habit, if you can give me half an hour." It took every ounce of control to keep her voice light to prevent another angry outburst.

He was all pleasant smiles and joviality again. "Yes, yes, of course, cousin." Then he looked to Gran. "Grandmother." He nodded stiffly and left the room.

Neither Venetia nor Gwen spoke right away, waiting until the sound of booted steps down the hall assured them that Patrick was out of hearing.

"Good heavens." Venetia wrapped her arms around herself.

"You will not go riding with them. I will not allow it," Gwen declared.

Venetia rubbed her trembling arms and after a moment reached out to take her grandmother's hand in hers. "Gran, I must. And while I'm gone, you will see to it that we are packed and ready to leave for the country."

"I don't want you alone with them. He could

arrange to have his friend compromise you, or worse. For all we know, that man has a priest waiting there as well."

It was a valid concern, but Venetia thought—or rather, hoped—Patrick was not that desperate yet.

Venetia dropped her arms to her sides and clenched her fists. "I am four and twenty. I have no need to let anyone force me into marriage simply out of a desire to avoid scandal. Society can hang itself."

Her father had warned her before her first season that men usually did not like intelligent wives, nor wives who wanted to be considered a partner rather than a servant within the marriage. He'd warned her that many men would say pleasing things, and promise the moon, but that once married, she would find her wings clipped like a songbird trapped in a cage.

The thought had so frightened her at seventeen that Venetia had happily avoided all but the most necessary appearances during her first season. She'd garnered no suitors due to her almost hermit-like behavior, but that had been her intention. It was better to be alone than to sacrifice her happiness simply to marry.

Gwen sighed heavily. "My dear, listen to an old woman when she tells you that men like Patrick are dangerous, especially when they believe they stand no chance of getting what they want through civility. You must never assume you are safe from his schemes. Forced marriages can be achieved, and men of the cloth can be bribed. No, I think we must find a solution, but I know you will make a fuss over it when I speak it."

Sudden realization of her grandmother's intentions made Venetia shake her head frantically. "No, no, no, Gran."

"Yes, my dear. It's time we find you a husband. One who is up to scratch, and one of your own choosing, of course. But more importantly, one who can give Patrick a good thrashing when we need him to." She whipped her cane in the air as though whacking an invisible Patrick on the head.

"You know my feelings on marriage. It is a trap, a devaluation of a woman's already limited independence."

"Yes, I know. But, Venetia, love, not all men are like that buffoon you call a cousin."

"He's your grandson," Venetia reminded Gwen.

"Yes, and his father, was such a good lad. It makes one wonder if the poor man was cuckolded, because that boy is a terrible creature, and I would do anything to disclaim a connection to him." Her grandmother covered Venetia's shoulders with a gentle arm. "Go riding if you must, and I will have all of our things packed before you return. We won't stay here another night, we'll move out at once. We'll go to the house party in the country, and I will find us a home elsewhere in London so that we won't have to return here. With your trust, we will be able to afford something quite suitable."

Venetia didn't want to leave this house. It was her home, not Patrick's, though she had no legal claim upon it. Patrick was free to tear it down to rubble if he so desired.

"How can we manage, Gran?" Venetia asked in a quiet voice. She didn't mean the question in matters of money. Patrick was their only male relative, and it would be expected that they would have some dealings with him, yet neither she nor Gwen desired that. Two women alone in society, the youngest soon to be an old spinster, although she hated the thought of men labeling her such when she felt neither old nor spinsterish. She felt as though the disapproving gaze of all London society would burn them to ash if they attempted to declare their independence from men.

"How can we manage?" Gwen gave her shoulder a squeeze. "Because we're *Dunham* ladies. We stand tall in the face of adversity. We may bend when we must, but we never break."

Venetia tried to find a smile, but it never found her lips. She left the drawing room and headed to her bedchamber to change into her riding habit. She found her lady's maid, Phoebe Upton, sorting out gowns on her bed. She was relieved not to have to ring the bell. Patrick had been attempting to reduce the staff, and Gran fought him on the matter frequently. He'd already terminated several of the upstairs maids, even though he was not the one who paid for their services. Each time this happened, Gran left the house to find the servants and bring them back. All of the servants now dreaded the ring of any upstairs bell. For them it had come to toll their employment doom. It was another reminder that it was time to leave this house and escape its great unhappiness.

"Afternoon, my lady." Phoebe smiled. She was a lovely woman in her late thirties, and an experienced servant Venetia had trusted for years with the secrets of her heart.

"Would you retrieve my riding habit, Phoebe? I am to go out with Lord Latham."

Phoebe halted abruptly before she reached the armoire. "You're what?" Phoebe demanded, then apparently realized she'd overstepped and cleared her throat. "That is to say, what could he have offered to make that worth doing?"

Venetia sat down at her vanity table and buried her face in her hands. She pressed hard against her closed eyelids until she saw flashes of white. Then she breathed deeply and faced her maid.

"I am buying us time, Phoebe. We are to quit this place. While I ride this afternoon, you are to assist the dowager countess with packing as much as you can."

"Now that makes far more sense," Phoebe muttered. "Best to leave that man far behind." The maid continued to mutter vigorously as she helped Venetia change into a blue riding habit with black braided frogging. When they finished, Venetia put her train over one arm and returned downstairs. Patrick was pacing at the entranceway, slapping his brown riding gloves against his palms. The harsh action of that single movement belied his congenial smile.

"There you are. We are running late. I told Bernard we would meet him at half past two."

"I'm so sorry," Venetia apologized, though she didn't mean it at all. She forced a smile so genuine that Gwen would have been proud.

"Shall we be off? I had the horses brought round."

"Of course." Venetia was helped into the saddle by one of the grooms, and then they headed for Hyde Park, which thankfully was not far.

Venetia had not met many of Patrick's friends. Between being in mourning for the last year and the fact that Patrick clearly preferred his club for socialization than with her and Gran, it meant they shared no social circles at all. Given Patrick's choice of friends, it was no doubt a blessing to avoid any connections with the majority of them.

"Ah, there he is." Patrick pointed at a distant rider at the opening to the park. A man astride a roan gelding waved his crop at them. Venetia tried to keep calm and remember that Patrick would not attempt some scheme in such a public place. He was a fool, but he was not stupid. Still, Venetia kept a tight grip on her riding crop. She would use it as a whip if they tried to manhandle her.

"Hello, Bernard. May I present my fair cousin, Venetia? Venetia, Mr. Bernard Kenyon."

The man, not unpleasant in looks, offered her a dangerous smile. "It is indeed my greatest pleasure to meet you. Patrick has done nothing but sing your praises. I find his description of you falls quite short, however. He failed to mention your sunny-colored hair or those rich doe-brown eyes. You are quite enchanting."

Simpering compliments, just as her father had said. But beneath those compliments, what lay in Bernard's heart? Was he in league with her cousin to get her fortune? She'd wager anything that he was.

"Thank you, Mr. Kenyon. I am sure we shall become better acquainted in time, but if you do not mind, I would very much like to exercise my horse."

She gave the beast, a lovely white mare named Snow, a gentle pat on the neck, then urged the horse into a brisk trot. As much as she knew she needed to delay things to give Gran time to pack, she did not want this fortune hunter attempting to compose more false compliments. It made her uncomfortable. The two gentlemen soon caught up and settled on either side of her, which left her feeling distinctly trapped.

Do not panic, she reminded herself. But it was hard to convince her heart to listen. It was beating too fast, and an unwelcome heat flushed her cheeks as she soon became flustered. She tried to picture Gran marshaling the servants to pack faster, and a feeling of hope briefly distracted her from her rising panic.

"Will you be in London this fall?" Bernard asked her.

"Yes, of course." Another lie, but she carried it off beautifully. If she and Gran were successful, perhaps they could even purchase a place in the country for a year and avoid Patrick entirely.

"That is excellent news indeed. I have high hopes that you and I will see more of each other." Bernard offered her what she supposed was meant to be a charming grin. However, it was so clearly a performance that Venetia nearly cringed. She masked her reaction by fiddling with her reins.

"Would it not be lovely, cousin?" Patrick urged with a lift of his dark brows.

"Yes," she replied.

After Patrick's show of temper earlier, Venetia was quite sure he could do her and Gran a measure of harm if they were not careful. It was best to play along. For now.

"I heard that Lord and Lady Helmsley are hosting a ball in two days," Bernard said casually. But the measured pace of his announcement hinted that he had practiced it. "I would be honored to claim your first dance."

Venetia had been raised a lady and nearly every moment of her life had acted like one, but right then she had no desire at all to dance with him or anyone else. So she did the sensible—but unladylike—thing and promised she would when she had no intention of keeping that promise.

"See? What a lovely day this has been." Patrick leaned in closer to her to whisper with a smug smile. "I told you, Venetia, that I would see you married, and it will be soon." Despite his smile, his words dripped with poison.

Men truly did believe women were dolls to be moved about, dressed, played with, and put away until the mood suited them. Well, Venetia wouldn't allow it. She nearly growled in frustration but swallowed the urge. There was too much at stake.

As much as she didn't wish to agree with Patrick, she'd come to the sad conclusion that Gran was right.

The only way to be safe from Patrick's schemes was to marry, but someone of her choosing. Someone who would not threaten her, cage her, or strangle the life out of her by degrees over the decades.

But did such a man even exist? Someone who was kind, compassionate, and passionate, who believed in an equal partner in a marriage? If he did, she would do everything in her power to find him and marry him.

She smiled at Patrick, the expression laden with sugary sweetness. "Yes, I believe I will be married soon enough."

He thought he could browbeat her into submission? He was even more a fool than Gran had thought.

She kept the two men at the park for nearly an hour and a half, and while they were content to enjoy the ride further, she was not. She suddenly winced and bent over on her sidesaddle.

"Oh heavens," she exclaimed dramatically, calling the attention of both men.

"I say, are you all right, Lady Venetia?" Bernard inquired.

"I . . . Yes. That is to say . . . Oh, this is most distressing, but the matter is one of a feminine nature, and even telling you this much has caused me quite a bit of distress."

"A feminine nature?" Patrick said, then his eyes

widened with horror. "You must wish to return home at once."

"Yes, but please go on with your ride. It would only pain me further to make you witness my embarrassment by having you escort me home. It might become . . . unsightly."

Both men turned ruddy cheeked and looked bashfully away like schoolboys. Venetia held back a giggle. Leave it to men to run away at the first mention of anything connected to the feminine body that did not immediately lead to their own pleasure.

"By all means, go. We'll be fine, won't we, Bernard?"

"We certainly will." Bernard offered her a congenial smile. Venetia had to remind herself to act disappointed before she turned her horse in the opposite direction.

When she reached home, she found that her grandmother had managed much in such a short time. A large wagon was out front, loaded with at least a dozen trunks. Footmen were piling more small boxes upon it. Their coach sat behind the wagon, already prepared for them.

"Heavens, Gran has been busy," Venetia murmured as she rushed into the house. "Gran?" she called out.

"Up here, my dear." Gwen peered at her from the top of the stairs, cane in hand, but she was looking livelier than ever. Phoebe was ready to assist her down.

"I've already secured a townhouse to accommodate everything we don't need for the house party. Half the staff will move in to set up the house for us, it will be ready when we return from Hartland Abbey."

"How on earth did you find a townhouse so quickly?"

Gwen's eyes glinted with mischief. "When you are my age, you learn to plan. I secured the townhouse a week ago in case of such an emergency. I didn't tell you, my dear, because I didn't wish to worry you."

Gwen reached the bottom of the stairs, and Venetia caught her free hand, gently holding it. "No more secrets, Gran. Please. If we are to survive this, we need truth between us."

"No secrets? Child, half the fun in life lies in secrets. But yes, I'll agree to the spirit of those terms. Now come along. Phoebe and I were preparing the coach when you arrived. It's time we left for Hartland."

"Isn't the party two days away? Surely we cannot arrive earlier than expected."

"Yes, but we will need to stay at an inn on the way. We can extend our stay at the inn another day and then finish the journey to Hartland."

It seemed that Gran had planned for everything.

Venetia should have been relieved, but she wasn't. Her grandmother intended to see her good and married.

She just hoped Gran didn't intend for her to put expedience ahead of happiness.

2

Adrian Montague groaned as he was shaken awake by a gentle hand.

"It's half past five," a sleepy voice murmured, trailing off into a yawn.

Adrian sat up. "Christ." He raked his hands through his hair before glancing at Benjamin, one of the other footmen employed at Hartland Abbey. Their shared room had a pair of tiny wood-framed beds, one washstand, and a chest of drawers they split between them. Life in service meant everything was shared, right down to the livery clothes on his back.

He had been a footman at Hartland for ten years. Now nine and twenty, he was coming into the age where men like him would either move on or advance into an underbutler position. But he doubted that

Hartland's butler, Mr. Reeves, would consider him for the position. Not given his family history.

It was one thing to allow the bastard son of a duke to stand as a pretty decoration in livery, but it was quite another to let him move into a more prominent position within such a noble household. Mr. Reeves, while an affable and fatherly man to all employed at the Abbey, was not quite so free and forward as to propose such an idea to Lord Devon and his duchess, Lady Devon.

"Come on, Adrian. I smell breakfast. We'd better get a move on." Benjamin lit a candle in the dark interior of the basement room, giving them enough light to change into their uniforms of black breeches and gold-striped waistcoats.

When Adrian was dressed, he joined a few of the other lower staff as they ate a quick breakfast of toast and poached eggs. Then he accepted a tray for Mr. Reeves from the cook, Marion Webster.

"Best to wake up a bit, dear," Mrs. Webster teased and pinched his cheek, winning her a rare smile. Adrian had a soft spot for the old girl. She was the mother of Phillip Webster, the valet for the Duke of Devon's second-oldest son, William Hampton, or Lord William.

Adrian climbed the winding stairs to the ground floor to wake Mr. Reeves and to deliver his breakfast. It was going to be a long day for everyone belowstairs. The Abbey was to play host to a house party for the next week. Coaches would be arriving throughout the day. Everyone would need tending to, luggage carried, tea and food brought up, and new servants settled. He and the rest of the staff would not go to bed until well after midnight tonight.

He knocked lightly on Mr. Reeves's door, and the butler called for him to enter. He set the tray down on the small table beside the butler's bed.

"Morning, Adrian. Is everyone else up?"

"Yes, Mr. Reeves."

"Good. See that everyone is on schedule. I will confirm with Mrs. Miller as to the guest list. Make sure you and Benjamin watch the bells for coaches arriving."

"Yes, Mr. Reeves."

Adrian descended back down into the kitchens and dodged around sleepy-eyed upstairs maids, grooms, and a few of the upstairs servants, who were all starting their day.

Adrian knew all of them well, but he usually kept to himself, even though he counted many of them as friends. It was easier that way. The scandal of his birth could damage many of those around him. He was the bastard son of a duke, but not the Duke of Devon. No, the honor of his parentage was that of the Duke of Stratford, who had seduced his children's young governess after his wife had died. When society had discovered the affair, Stratford had been forced to send her north to bear the child in secret.

Adrian had lived with his mother in Northumberland until he was nineteen, doing his best to earn a living working in a local tavern. When his mother had died of a fever, he'd been left to make his way in the world alone.

He had gone to Stratford's home only once, bearing the letter his mother had written in her final hours. The duke had refused to see him. Instead, he'd been given a letter that he was not allowed to read and an address of where he was to go. That was how he had shown up on Lord Devon's doorstep, weary, hungry, in threadbare clothes, and desperate for work. Mr. Reeves had been skeptical of him, like any good butler would be, yet he still had delivered the letter from Lord Stratford to his master.

Adrian remembered how he'd wanted so desperately to be let inside and to rest. Half an hour later, Mr. Reeves had let him enter through the infamous green baize doorway that marked the servants' domain at Hartland Abbey. From that day to this, he had been welcomed by the other staff and had become a favorite of the house.

He was of an age close to the children of the house, and his attractive features, ones he had inherited from his mother, made him a talking piece of any visiting ladies and even a few men. His height, well over six feet, and his dark hair and amber eyes put him in a unique position—both intensely desirable and completely untouchable.

It was one thing for houseguests to partake in physical pleasures with one another, but servants could not engage with each other, let alone the guests. Adrian had only had a handful of lovers in the last few years, and all of those had been young women who lived and worked in the nearby village. Some had called him a heartbreaker, but he'd done his best to let each young woman down gently when it had been time to part ways.

A life in service was a lonely one, and Adrian felt that now more than ever as the coaches began to arrive. He stared almost forlornly at the first coach rattling down the road toward him. How many times had he stood there waiting for coaches like this? How many years would he continue to live here at the Abbey, answering the calls of the highborn gentry?

He and half a dozen other footmen, along with Mr. Reeves, stood ready to greet the first coach as it made a slow arc in front of the house and stopped before the door.

The coach was a lovely dark blue with bright yellow accents. Four horses pulled it, all matching bays of exquisite health and form. The stable master, Mr. Fredrickson, would be delighted to house such handsome beasts. Adrian had listened to him wax on about horses for hours at the servants' table on more than one night. The man knew good horseflesh when he saw it.

At a nod from Mr. Reeves, Adrian approached the coach door. He unfolded the step and turned the handle, ready to assist whoever came out.

A silver cane jutted out, followed by the silver hair of an older woman. She wore a dark-blue gown, much like the coach she rode in. She accepted Adrian's outstretched hand, and he was careful to assist her down once he realized that she was a rather delicate lady. The woman turned a pair of dark-brown eyes on him.

"Lord, I sometimes forget how handsome you devils are. Lady Devon has rather good taste in footmen, don't you agree?" This last comment was directed at whoever was inside the coach behind her.

Adrian remained impassive as the older woman released his hand and headed toward the house. He turned his attention to whoever was still inside and froze at the sight of a lovely blonde-haired creature with dark-brown eyes. Her face was flushed as she placed her gloved hand in his.

"Please forgive my grandmother. She is forthright at the best of times and can be quite impertinent when she knows she can get away with it." The young lady, for she was indeed younger than him, had a soft, sweet voice—neither too girlish nor too deep.

Adrian almost forgot to release her hand after she stepped down onto the ground. He wasn't used to guests speaking directly to him unless they were giving an order, and he certainly wasn't used to a pretty young lady talking to him.

"It is no trouble, my lady," Adrian replied quickly as he realized he had been staring at her and hadn't responded.

The young woman walked past him into the house, leaving him with visions of wildflowers and stolen kisses in the gardens at twilight. Lord, what would it be like to kiss a woman like her? He sighed softly, his gaze still on her as she vanished from view.

"Adrian, it would be best to put your eyes back inside your head," Mr. Reeves warned, but there was no real bite to the butler's tone. He knew Adrian had never broken his code of conduct as a servant of the house of Devon, and no matter how lovely that young lady was, he wouldn't start now.

But that didn't stop a man from indulging in a few wicked daydreams.

❧

GWEN GREETED A LOVELY WOMAN IN HER midforties as she and Venetia were shown into the drawing room. "Marrian!"

"Gwen!" The Duchess of Devon met Venetia and

her grandmother at the door with a warm hug. Lady Devon's blue eyes were warm as she held Venetia's hands. "You look so much like your mother. Heavens, I miss her dearly."

"As do I, Your Grace." Venetia had met Lady Devon only once as a child. Her mother and the duchess had spent much time together socially over the years, but Venetia had been too young to participate in such activities herself.

"You are such a dear to invite us," Gwen replied. "And if I am honest, you rather saved us."

Venetia blanched at her grandmother's open admission.

"What's all this now?" Lady Devon gestured for them to sit on the settee near the fireplace.

"Gran, Lady Devon doesn't need to hear about our—"

Gwen tapped her cane on the floor. "Nonsense. She certainly does need to hear it. She's the one woman in all of England I trust to help us find you a suitable husband."

Venetia was ready to perish on the spot with mortification.

"Oh? Are we husband hunting?" Lady Devon grinned. "This is delightful. Venetia, my dear, your mother had such wonderful hopes for you to make a brilliant match. It was such a tragedy that she did not live long enough to see you wed."

"Thank you, Lady Devon, but I am afraid that the notion of my marrying is a point of contention between myself and my grandmother at the moment. I would prefer to take my time in choosing a husband."

"It certainly is not a point of contention," Gwen grumbled. "Marrian, tell her that I am right. My scheming grandson wishes to gain access to Venetia's assets by marrying her off to one of his friends. I won't allow it."

Lady Devon gasped and turned to Venetia. "Is this true?"

"Well, yes, but I told Gran that no one can force me to marry."

At this Lady Devon and Gwen exchanged looks, then turned back to her. "If the world were a just place, you would be right. But this is a world made for men. A determined man can force you to marry, and should you claim foul afterward, such a man might have you declared mad and send you away. Unfortunately, your safest course of action is to marry someone of your choosing, someone you like and trust."

Gwen harrumphed in agreement. "Exactly. We need to find a strapping, handsome young buck who can throw Patrick out on his ear if he even breathes disrespectfully around Venetia."

Lady Devon chuckled. "I'm not sure who would

fit that description, but the night is young." She rang a bell for tea, and a footman entered, placing the tea tray on the table beside Lady Devon.

Normally Venetia would not look at servants. It wasn't out of a sense of superiority, but rather deference to their need to be unseen. But she couldn't help but notice that he was the same dark-haired footman who had assisted her down from the coach. She had apologized to him for her grandmother's conduct, and he had held her hand a moment too long.

His eyes were a delightful shade of brown and hazel that reminded her of amber. He was devastatingly handsome, with a strong chin, and his lashes, too long for a man, made him seem almost pretty. He was broad-shouldered and impossibly tall, at least a foot and a half above her. Gran would have called him an Adonis.

His eyes were downcast as he set the tray on the table. He was so close that she could smell leather and something softer upon him, a bit of sandalwood perhaps. His proximity sent her blood humming.

The footman straightened and backed away. For a brief moment, his eyes flicked toward her, as though he wanted to steal a glance and didn't expect her to be watching him. The flare of heat in his eyes answered the call of her own.

That single ephemeral connection nearly made

her gasp. It was only by the grace of God that neither Lady Devon nor Gran noticed.

Baffled, Venetia tried to focus on the conversation, but all she could think about was how she'd never felt like this around any man before. It was one of the reasons she'd so easily dismissed desire and love as a component of marriage. Because until that moment, she'd never felt such attraction before.

This stirring of hope, so new, like a fledgling bird, had nowhere to go but to plummet to its death upon the ground. This perfect Adonis was a footman, after all. A domestic servant in the employ of Lady Devon. Stealing him away as a husband would be considered a cardinal sin. The unfortunate truth was that he was lowborn. Though she despised that phrase immensely, and would be content to tell society to hang if they dared to voice their opinions on her choice of husband, any children they had would be subjected to the cruelties of others whispering about their parents.

But even thinking of this was silly. Venetia was still hoping to avoid matrimony if at all possible, and a fine pair of shoulders and a face to make angels weep was not something she should be obsessing over. Her father had raised her to be a strong, independent woman, and he had created the financial trust to protect her as best he could.

The truth was, once she was married, most of her

money would belong to her husband, for good or ill. Venetia could not ever imagine trusting any man with that power over her and Gran's future.

Lady Devon tapped her chin in thought before pouring their cups of tea. "I believe Lord Essex might make a good match. He's twenty-nine, dark-haired, stunning green eyes, a bit brooding perhaps—but oh wait, he has a mistress, some French creature. No, that won't do."

"Best to stay away from any man with a mistress," Gran added. "I want a loyal man for Venetia. She won't take to just any randy young buck who makes a good ride. She needs steadiness, faithfulness."

Venetia was about to interrupt and tell Lady Devon that Gran didn't make all of her decisions, when they were all distracted by an odd noise.

There was a choking sound outside the open drawing room door, and the afternoon sunlight illuminated the shadow of the footman lingering in his appropriate place, within hearing distance should his mistress need him.

Gwen paused at the choking sound but then continued. "As I was saying, looks aren't enough. So, what young men do you have in mind whom Venetia might sample this week?"

Lady Devon burst into laughter. "Oh heavens, Gwen, I always forget how much I adore you. But Venetia cannot *sample* men—they aren't fruit tarts.

She must study them, converse with them, see if there is a natural attraction. *Sampling* makes it sound as though you expect her to tuck them away in the alcoves after dinner for stolen kisses so she might compare them later on."

Gwen played with her cane. "That might be yet what the child needs. She's never been suitably courted. A kiss goes quite a way to tell how a man might perform his marital duties. Will he sweep her off her feet? Bore her with a chaste and brotherly kiss? Or slobber over her like some odious hound?"

Again, the poor footman outside was choking, and this time it was so distracting that Gwen stood.

"You there, footman. Come in here and have a cup of tea before you perish." Gwen turned to Lady Devon. "That's all right with you, isn't it? The poor man's face is bright red, and I do believe he needs it."

Lady Devon turned to look over her shoulder toward the doorway. "Adrian, do come in and have some tea if you need it."

The footman, Adrian, slipped back into the room, red-faced and still coughing as he hastily collected his drink and tried to dash back into the hall, but Gwen was too fast. She thrust her cane out, rapping at his chest and bringing him to a halt.

"See, this is what I'm looking for, Marrian. A lovely, handsome young buck, but a respectful and polite one."

"But not a footman, surely," Lady Devon said with a chuckle. "Though I must admit, Adrian is rather dashing, isn't he? Oh, do forgive us, Adrian. We ladies are most rude, aren't we? Speaking of your gender as if you were horseflesh. Please take your tea and return to your post. If Mr. Reeves gets on you, I shall have a word with him."

With a bashful glance at the three ladies, the handsome footman vanished into the hall. Venetia watched him go and was still staring at his shadow outside as her grandmother coughed politely to get her attention.

"So, you do have a type of man after all," Gwen mused, giving a smile that meant trouble for Venetia. "Dark hair and fine eyes? Well, I shall make a note of that, my dear. You shall have only the best." Gwen walked back to her couch and sat down with a smugness that ordinarily would have left Venetia giggling. But the current situation was too dire to find even a tiny bit of this amusing.

"So, Marrian, tell us who we can expect to arrive this evening."

Venetia rose and made her apologies to Lady Devon and Gran before excusing herself from the room. The footman was gone and the hall was empty. That was a small relief. She wasn't sure she could face him after her grandmother's inappropriate comments.

She wandered through the house until she found a pair of terrace doors that led outside. She took in the fresh air with relief and walked toward the distant gardens. Only then did she have a moment to enjoy Hartland Abbey. It reminded her of her beloved family's country home, Latham House, the one Patrick had so callously sold only a month after her father had been laid to rest.

Hartland was a vision from a dream. Bathed in sunlight, the house hovered at the end of a golden autumn glade, its architecture frozen in time, the trees casting long, glorious shadows upon the well-tended lawns. The scent of fruit hung heavy in the air, and distant orchards at the far end of the garden lured visitors with their sweetness. The flowers along the walking path were drenched with a heavy dew that only now was starting to fade. Venetia adored life in a country house. This quiet world was full of golden joys, and moonlit winters were eternally present. Life and its inherent stresses were happily avoided here.

Turning down another path, she wandered out into a field to admire the vista. With an impulsive shriek of delight, she lifted her skirts and sprinted down the hill. She reached the bottom in just a few minutes and laughed with silly delight as she spun in circles and then collapsed on the ground to stare up at the clouds.

She must have dozed off in that sunny meadow because she woke to the prickling of wet, cold rain upon her face. She bolted upright and noted, with no small amount of shock, the rolling waves of rain rising up from the distant valley toward her.

She scrambled to her feet and started to run. She had made it halfway up the hill when the rain struck, and the once welcoming hillside turned treacherously slick. She slipped, scrabbling against the steep hill, and cried out as her ankle turned sharply. She felt a horrifying pop. She collapsed, her mind blank with numbing pain. She had no breath to even scream.

She rolled over onto her back, every muscle now seized with violent pain. Her mouth stretched in a silent scream until she lay shivering hard enough to rattle her teeth. All she could think about was the pain in her ankle. She could not stand, and she could not walk in the rain, which was now falling in heavy torrential waves across the field.

3

"I s there a reason you are drinking from one of Her Grace's teacups?" Mr. Reeves's disapproving tone jolted Adrian from his thoughts. He hastily lowered the teacup.

"I . . . I had a coughing fit, Mr. Reeves. Her Grace invited me to drink so that it might relieve it."

Mr. Reeves raised a dark brow, his hazel eyes quite severe and his expression most stern. "I suggest you take that down to the kitchen at once and have it washed. Then have Mrs. Webster make you tea in a more appropriate cup."

"Yes, sir." Adrian left his position outside the drawing room, but Mr. Reeves's admonishment was already forgotten. He was lost in dreams of that lovely young woman. He hadn't been able to avoid overhearing the duchess and her guests' conversation. The older woman, the Dowager Countess of Latham, was quite a firebrand. He liked spirit in a woman of any age, and humor even more. It was why he had choked on his own stifled laughter when she had been discussing her criteria in a man suitable for her granddaughter.

Adrian would have loved to be the man for Lady Venetia. She was exquisite. There were others who could be considered more beautiful, perhaps, but there was a kindness in Lady Venetia's face and a genuineness about her that was appealing. She was shy, it seemed, yet openhearted. She was easy to read and yet not simpleminded as some ladies could be.

Not that he had any right to think of Lady Venetia in such a way. She was the daughter of an earl, a finely bred gentlewoman. No matter what he wanted, Lady Venetia could give nothing to him, not her heart, and not her body. She shone bright like a winter star. Brilliant, beautiful, and very much out of reach.

Adrian sank into a chair at the servants' table near the kitchen in the basement of the house. He still held Lady Devon's dainty white-and-blue china teacup. Lord William's valet, Phillip Webster, was seated across from him, a polishing cloth in one hand and a boot in the other.

"Adrian, are you all right?" Phillip asked.

"What? Oh yes, I'm all right."

Phillip grinned. "Having tea with Her Grace?" He nodded at the cup.

"No," he chuckled. "But Mr. Reeves thought so. I'll be paying for that, I'm sure."

"He'll make you polish the silver teapots again," Phillip guessed.

"Probably." Adrian laughed and then winced. The elaborate silver teapots were hard to polish because of the intricate metalwork that allowed the tarnish to set in deeply. Any servant who had been on Mr. Reeves's bad side was often relegated to this task as punishment.

"Is your mother ready for the party this week?" Adrian asked the valet.

"Oh yes, I think so. She's been gushing over her planned menus with Lady Devon and Mrs. Miller for the last two days. The upstairs crowd will be dining well, that's for certain."

Adrian sighed and got back on his feet. "Don't they always?" It was time to return upstairs.

He had just entered the grand entryway when the Dowager Countess of Latham exited the drawing room.

"Ah, you again, young man. Come here." She rapped her cane on the floor like a king, summoning him.

"Yes, your ladyship?" Adrian kept hands behind his back in a respectful stance.

"Do you know where my granddaughter is?"

"I'm afraid I do not, but I would be happy to find her for you."

"Yes, please do that. I will be in my chambers." Lady Latham nodded at him like a general, then proceeded up the stairs. She moved quickly for someone who appeared so frail.

Adrian spent the next quarter of an hour searching for Lady Venetia. It wasn't until he found one of the grooms, who said he'd seen her in the gardens, that Adrian believed he knew where to find her.

"Lady Venetia?" He called out her name as he explored the towering maze of hedgerows and the flowering walkways. He checked the orchard next as heavy storm clouds rumbled overhead. The rain, it seemed, had passed, which left him wondering where the young lady was. He was positive she wasn't inside the Abbey, because no one had seen her. So where—?

A distant cry caught his attention. It came from behind the gardens, deep into the meadow that sloped down to the valley below the Abbey. He thought that one of the sheep, possibly a young ewe, had become stranded in the rain. He wiped his face with his sleeve and stripped out of his coat in case he needed to carry the distressed animal to the nearest tenant farm. He crossed the meadow and reached the spot where the hills sloped down, and then he halted. A creature lay huddled halfway down the slope, but the distressed creature was not a lamb—it was a young lady.

"Hello there! I'm coming down!" He started to run, but the young lady shouted for him to stop.

"Please, be careful. It's very slick!" she cried out.

Adrian checked himself and found as he proceeded more cautiously that she was indeed right. The rain had sluiced down the golden grass, forming a treacherous path. It took him a few minutes to reach her.

"My lady," he gasped as he realized she was Lady Venetia. Her gown, once a bright blue, was now darkened with rain and clung to her form, teasing him with far too much of a view of her curves.

He knelt beside her. Her face was tight with pain and white as a sheet. "Are you able to walk?"

"I am not sure, Mr. . . ."

"Montague. But please, call me Adrian. May I see?" He pointed to her ankle. She nodded but did not move. He raised her skirts up to her calves and assessed her legs. He tried not to notice just how fine they were and felt like a bounder for noticing anyway. Her right ankle was swelling, however, and likely would swell much more by this evening.

"I can carry you, my lady." He started to reach for her, but she shook her head.

"It isn't safe. At least, not on the hill."

"Why don't we get you on your feet? I can put my arm around your waist, and you can lean on me. We should be able to climb the hill if we move carefully enough."

"Yes, all right." Her brown eyes grew wide as he put his arms around her back and lifted her up against him to stand. Her hands fluttered against his chest.

"Lean on me, and I'll be able to hold you up." She weighed little, and as soon as he had them safely on top of the hill, he planned to carry her whether she liked it or not.

"I'm ready," Lady Venetia said.

"All right." He put her by his side and kept one arm around her back and under her arms, then lifted her. She made not one sound of pain, though she swayed into him, her wet skin chilly against his when her face brushed against his neck. Her body trembled as she tried to hobble one step forward.

"I cannot put any weight down," Lady Venetia whispered.

"Hold on to me, sweetheart," Adrian murmured, not even pausing to think about his breach of etiquette. Mr. Reeves would do more than have him polish silver teapots if he ever heard about it.

They moved up the hill, slow step by slow step, and Adrian held on to her tightly, afraid of doubling her pain if she were to stumble again. When they reached the top of the hill and Hartland Abbey with its rain-soaked gardens came into view, he let out a breath he hadn't realized he'd been holding.

"The ground is even now. Allow me to carry you the rest of the way, my lady."

She bit her lip and seemed ready to protest, but before she could answer, he swept her up into the cradle of his arms.

Lady Venetia put her arms around his neck, her breathing shallow as she held tightly to him. After years of carrying heavy trunks up and down the stairs for guests, carrying this petite woman was an easy task. He had no trouble doubling his pace once he was on flat land. They were halfway into the gardens when Phillip and Benjamin rushed to meet them.

"Good God!" Phillip muttered. "What the devil happened?"

"There was an accident," Adrian cut in. Lady Venetia looked even more upset. "We need the doctor. She might have a broken ankle."

"I'll fetch the doctor and tell Mr. Reeves," Benjamin said.

Phillip opened the terrace doors for Adrian. "Let me help you get her settled in, then I'll find her maid."

"Phoebe," Venetia murmured in a slightly dazed voice. "Phoebe is my maid."

"Yes, of course," Phillip said.

Adrian carried Venetia up the stairs and into the east wing, where her bedchamber was located. Phillip opened the door, and Adrian eased the lady down upon the bed, then he left to go find Phoebe. Her clothing was soaked clear through, her teeth still chattering. Adrian knew he was supposed to wait for her maid, but the longer they waited, the more Venetia risked illness.

"My lady, at the risk of losing my employment here, I believe we need to undress you. Those clothes are drenched, and you could catch a chill. As soon as your maid arrives, I will leave, but please let me help you remove some of the clothing."

Venetia nodded and fumbled for the buttons on her pelisse. Adrian pushed her hands away and made quick work of the buttons. Then he peeled the dark-blue velvet pelisse off her arms. It hit the floor with a wet slapping sound. He then carefully removed her slippers to avoid hurting her swollen ankle.

"It was very foolish of me. I fell asleep in the meadow," she whispered, shivering in a way that made his heart clench with concern.

"It wasn't foolish, my lady," he reassured her as his hands stroked her calves while he rolled down her stockings. She was cold to the touch, yet her eyes were heated as she looked up at him in quiet surprise.

"You're very gentle," she said, as though confused by her own statement.

"Of course, my lady. One should always be gentle with a woman."

"I wish I knew more about men." This last statement was uttered so quietly that he thought perhaps he'd misheard her.

Adrian moved away from her to hang the stockings to dry. A moment later, Lady Venetia's maid burst in.

"My lady!" Phoebe rushed straight to Venetia and didn't notice Adrian laying the stockings on the top of the fire grate to dry them.

"Oh, Phoebe, you will laugh at me. It was so very silly. I slipped on the grass and hurt my ankle." All of this was spoken through Lady Venetia's chattering teeth and shivering lips.

"I would never laugh." Phoebe began undoing the laces of the gown as she rolled her mistress over. Adrian froze at the sight of Lady Venetia's body being bared to him.

"Thank you . . . Adrian," Venetia said drowsily at him.

Phoebe whirled and gasped. "What the devil are you doing here? Out with you! Out!" She chased

Adrian from the room and slammed the door. Phillip was waiting for him outside, half grinning.

"Saw a bit more of the lady than you should have, eh?"

Adrian chuckled. "Definitely more than I should have, but the lady was going to catch a chill, and I wasn't sure how quickly you would find her maid."

"Mr. Reeves will have you cleaning teapots for the next century, no matter that you saved the poor woman."

"I'm afraid my heroic actions will likely go unpraised." He chuckled wryly at the idea of anyone thinking him a hero.

"Most of the guests are here. Why don't you dry off and see to the rest of the luggage. I'll make sure Benjamin and the doctor find her."

Adrian clapped Phillip on the back and returned downstairs, only to run straight into Lady Latham.

"I've only just heard, you found my granddaughter outside and carried her into the house. What happened to her?" She held her cane tight, knuckles white, but he still heard the fear in her imperious tone.

"She slipped on the hill and twisted her ankle very badly, my lady. We sent for the doctor, and she is resting in her room."

"Thank you, Mr. . . . ," Lady Latham said more quietly.

"Adrian Montague, my lady."

"Adrian, yes, now I remember. Thank you. Venetia is my world, you see. If anything happened to her . . ."

"She's a strong young lady, and brave," Adrian said. "I'm sure she will be fine." He started to move around Lady Latham, but her cane rose as if of its own volition and blocked his passing.

"I shall make this known to Lady Devon. If it isn't too much trouble to ask, in addition to your other duties, would you be able to look after Lady Venetia? See that she has whatever she needs? I trust you, young man, and frankly, I like the look of you. It would do my stubborn little dear some good to spend time around a handsome young man with manners."

"Surely you don't mean for her to spend time with me?" She had to be forgetting that he was only a footman. Perhaps it was because he had left his coat out in the gardens.

"I'm aware that you are a servant, but that is merely a word to me. What matters is what is in here." She tapped his chest with her cane. "I will speak to Lady Devon. She may reduce your duties so you may care for Venetia."

Adrian didn't dare argue. "Yes, my lady." He bowed respectfully and let her pass by him to go up the stairs to see to her granddaughter. She disappeared down the hall, and he headed back out onto the terrace and into the rain to find his livery coat.

He tried to focus on how he would handle the butler's displeasure and not about how he might be spending more time than was wise with the beautiful Lady Venetia. Adrian was no rakehell, but even he would have to be on his best behavior around someone so sweet, or he would lose his home here and any reference that could see him settled elsewhere.

Lady Latham had no idea what she was asking of him.

❧

VENETIA WAS AWARE OF HER MAID'S MUTTERINGS AS she was stripped of the rest of her clothes and bundled into a clean, dry chemise. Her hair was combed out and the pins removed so the wet locks could dry faster.

"Damned man, touching your stockings." Phoebe herself was tweaking the damp stockings into a better hanging position on the fire grate. "The nerve of him."

"Please, Phoebe, do not be angry with him. He rescued me. I was the silly fool who fell down a hill. He carried me back to the house."

Her maid glanced her way. "Aye, like Lord bloody Byron he did, all that dark hair and fetching looks. Yes, he'd play the hero for any woman, I'm sure."

Venetia didn't like that her maid was so set against the footman. She cut off the maid's tirade. "He did me a great service, and it isn't his fault that he is rather dashing. Ladies of great houses always try to have the most attractive men in such positions."

Venetia let out a sneeze and fell back on the pillows. Her maid was there in an instant, cooing to her and handing her a cup of herbal tea. She wasn't really upset with Phoebe. Her maid was fiercely loyal and protective, often to a fault.

"There now, my lady." She fluffed the pillow, and Venetia drifted off to sleep until the doctor arrived. When she opened her eyes, she found her grandmother sitting beside her bed, watching with concern as the doctor examined Venetia's ankle.

The doctor was a man of middle age, and he had a pair of silver-rimmed spectacles perched on his nose. He tested her swollen ankle with gentle fingers.

"This will hurt, my lady, but I need to see if the ankle is broken." He rotated the joint slowly, and Venetia swallowed back a cry of pain.

"Thank heavens, 'tis only sprained, but I commend you," the doctor said. "You managed to pop the bone out of place and back in. That is far more painful than if you had broken it. But the good news is this means your recovery will be a few days rather than several weeks."

"That is good news," Gwen replied.

Her grandmother was unusually quiet. Normally she would be talking with the doctor about a great many things, but instead she was very subdued.

"Drink herbal tea, and stay warm and in bed for the next several days. I want you to send for me if you develop a fever. The valet who met me at the door said you'd been in the rain for some time. I wouldn't want you to catch a cold." He collected his hat and bag and bid Venetia and Gwen farewell.

When he'd gone, Venetia groaned. "So much for the house party. It seems I shall spend the entire time trapped in bed like some invalid."

"Do not fret, my dear. I'll see that you have company."

"Company? You won't keep me company?"

Gwen laughed. "No, my dear, not me. I am too old to keep you entertained for an entire week. No, that handsome footman will do nicely."

"What? Gran, that's not wise and certainly not proper."

Gwen smiled coyly. "Oh, come now. Life needs to be a bit improper at times. And this is a chance for you to learn how to be around young men. Your father kept you so protected that you've never had a decent opportunity for interaction. But don't worry, it's time we fix that."

"Gran," Venetia warned, but she was too tired and

her muscles still ached from when she'd fallen. There was little fight left in her.

Gwen kissed her forehead and patted her cheek. "Rest, my dear."

Despite her exhaustion, Venetia couldn't help but think about the disaster that would surely follow if she and Adrian were forced to be in each other's company for a week. However, she couldn't deny that her traitorous heart gave a few quickened beats at the thought.

He had been so romantic, looming out of the rain to lift her up, his warm hard body pressed tightly to hers. Their bodies had strained as they had moved up the hill as one, together, united. The thought brought a heated blush that would have sent Phoebe calling for the doctor had she been there. Venetia closed her eyes, remembering Adrian holding her. She could even still smell a hint of his scent upon her skin, the scent of man and cold rain mixed in an enticing blend. Had she ever noticed a man's scent beyond the usual overdone colognes at balls? Not really.

Gran was right—she could use more time around men, especially alone. There was so much she hadn't really thought would affect her, and she needed to be prepared for courtship. The footman would be good practice. Gran was also right about the fact that Venetia did have a soft spot for dark-haired men with fine eyes.

At least, eyes that belonged to a certain footman.

❦

GWEN FOUND LADY DEVON IN ONE OF THE drawing rooms, greeting a new group of guests. Once those guests had departed and she was alone with Lady Devon, Gwen took her chance.

"How is poor Venetia? I've only just heard what happened." Marrian was pale and wide-eyed with concern.

"Not a broken ankle, thank heavens. But she suffered a rather nasty sprain. She'll need to be in bed most of the week."

"Oh, how terribly disappointing," Marrian sighed. "I was so looking forward to matchmaking her with one of the gentlemen this week."

"As was I, but I believe we may still have some measure of success. I wasn't jesting when I said Venetia has never been properly courted. She's had no real opportunities for romance or attraction before. She was kept at a careful distance from most eligible men by my son, God rest him. I believe he feared that she would leave him if she were to marry, and after he lost her mother, he could not bear the thought. Then, when he passed, she was caught in a year of mourning. It is only now that she has a chance to taste life for the first time."

Lady Devon listened to her friend intently. "I imagine you have a plan, Gwen?"

"Actually, I do. That footman, the handsome one who seems to have trouble swallowing. The choking one, I mean."

"Oh, Adrian? Yes?"

"Would you think it horrid of me to request that he tend to her while she's recovering?"

"By *tend to her*, what do you mean?" Lady Devon asked.

"Bring her meals, eat with her, read to her, keep her company."

The duchess's brow furrowed. "You and I would keep quiet on the matter, but the servants, even the best of them, would talk. It's improper, and it would ruin her."

"Not if we have her maid present."

"Gwen, you don't even know Adrian. How could you trust him to be alone with her?"

Gwen smiled. "I trust him because you do. You and your husband only hire the best, and that young man has been with you a long time."

"He has," Lady Devon admitted. A flush to her cheeks caught Gwen's attention.

"But there's more to him than that, isn't there?" she asked cautiously. "Who is he, Marrian? Footmen do not make a duchess blush, not without cause."

Lady Devon looked away. "I shouldn't speak of it.

It isn't my place. Adrian is a wonderful young man, and you are right, he has worked hard in my home for ten years without one incident or word spoken against him."

Gwen knew she had touched upon something important about the footman, but now was not the time to press the matter. She needed Lady Devon to agree to let the man attend to Venetia.

"So you agree to this, then? You'll allow him to tend to her?"

"I . . . Well, I suppose so. So long as Mr. Reeves is not desperately in need of him."

Gwen hastened to assent to this. "Yes, of course, by all means."

"I will speak to Mr. Reeves privately and have his assurance to let Adrian see to this temporary position."

"Excellent." Gwen, cane in hand, headed for the door, but Lady Devon caught her arm gently.

"What if this goes too far? What if Venetia were to fall for him? You should be ready to face a broken-hearted grandchild should she become too attached."

"I know, it is a risk. But Venetia is a highborn lady. She knows she cannot marry below her station. I shall be ready to face the consequences, whatever they may be."

"So long as you are prepared," Lady Devon said.

Indeed, Gwen was prepared. She had seen desire

for a man in Venetia's eyes for the first time, and depending on what she could uncover about this young footman, perhaps . . .

But no. Venetia could never marry a man who was a servant. Society would shun her, and any children she might bear would suffer greatly. Still, Gwen had always loved to break the rules. Perhaps her grand-daughter would be brave enough to do the same.

4

"Adrian, Mr. Reeves is looking for you," Benjamin called out as Adrian finished drying off and brushing his coat. He had managed to use the flat iron to press the wrinkles from the rain out of the fabric, but it still smelled vaguely of a rainy field. Not an unpleasant scent, but it was noticeable, and Mr. Reeves would certainly be displeased with that.

"Did you say Mr. Reeves is looking for me?" he asked.

"Yes. You are to report to his office." Benjamin paused as he carried a tray of sandwiches past him toward the servants' stairs that led up to the main part of the house.

Adrian had an uncomfortable feeling about this. "What for?"

"I have no idea, but he is waiting for you."

Adrian stole a bite of turkey and porridge before he headed to reach Mr. Reeves's office and knocked.

"Come in," Mr. Reeves said.

Adrian slipped in and closed the door behind him only to freeze at the sight of Lady Devon standing next to the butler.

"Adrian, thank you for coming." The duchess beamed at him. Surely her smile meant he wasn't about to be tossed out.

He bowed his head. "Your ladyship."

"Adrian, I've spoken with her ladyship, and she wishes for you to have a special duty during the house party."

"A special duty, sir?" Adrian couldn't imagine what the butler was talking about.

Lady Devon laid a hand on Mr. Reeves's arm and spoke to Adrian directly.

"Lady Venetia has a terribly swollen ankle and must be resting in bed. Her grandmother, Lady Latham, has expressed her desire for you to attend to her this week."

"Yes, your ladyship," Adrian replied without thinking, stunned by the request. "What would my exact duties be?"

"Bring her meals, see that she has everything she needs." The duchess hesitated before turning to the butler. "Reeves, would you mind letting me have a moment alone with Adrian?"

The old butler squared his shoulders. "Of course, my lady." He bowed to her and arched a brow at Adrian before he left the room.

When the door closed, the duchess sighed. "I know this request is quite unconventional."

Adrian had been taught to hold his tongue, but he had questions that needed answers. "Pardon me, your ladyship, but does this have to do with the conversation from earlier today? I did not mean to overhear."

"Yes," the duchess said, and she actually relaxed. "I know it must have been impossible not to hear Lady Latham and her . . . unusual comments. Yes, I'm glad to speak freely of it. The truth is, Lady Venetia does need a bit of . . . Oh heavens, the word *experience* sounds very improper, but I suppose it is the most apt. She has been quite sheltered, not intellectually but romantically. And she is in need of a husband, and soon. It is important that she learns what a good man has to offer so she might know what to look for when choosing one. Lady Latham and I agree that you would suit very well for Venetia to have some interaction without the burden of the social situation." Lady Devon clasped her hands together. "Is it terrible to ask this of you?"

Adrian found a smile forming on his lips. "You've asked me to spend the week with a lovely and kind young woman. I do not see any hardship in the request and would be happy to do whatever you wish."

Lady Devon sighed in relief. "Thank you. I will make sure Reeves is made aware of how pleased you have made me."

"Thank you, your ladyship."

Adrian waited for the duchess to leave the room first, and then he followed her. Mr. Reeves was hovering in the corridor, scowling.

"So, you are to attend to Lady Venetia?"

"To be a companion of sorts, yes."

The butler harrumphed and muttered darkly about the impropriety of the entire situation, but Adrian knew the man wasn't angry with him.

"Well, let's start you off then. Go and see if Mrs. Webster has a tray of food and take it up to Lady Venetia's chambers."

"Yes, sir."

Adrian went to the kitchens, collected the tray, and began the long climb up the servants' stairs to the second floor, where Lady Venetia was resting. He knocked on her door, and her lady's maid, Phoebe, was already frowning at him.

"They sent you to entertain her, did they?"

"Er . . . Yes, I suppose."

"Well, you'd better come in, then."

"Who is it, Phoebe?" Venetia asked.

"Your footman." Phoebe took the tray from him and set it down on the table, leaving Adrian unsure of himself. He stayed just inside the door.

"Phoebe, would you see how Gran is doing? I worry when I cannot see her."

"My lady, I do not think I should leave you alone."

"Please, Phoebe. I will be fine."

Phoebe gave Adrian an *I am watching your every move* scowl and left the bedchamber.

"Please forgive her. Phoebe is most protective of me. She has been my maid since I was fifteen."

"I understand, my lady."

"Venetia. Won't you please call me that? Since my grandmother has made you come to attend me, could we not have a friendship during this week? It would do much to alleviate my guilt about taking you away from your other duties."

She shifted beneath the bed's counterpane, and Adrian became all too aware that this beautiful lady lying in bed in her underclothes was only a few feet from him. The thought made every muscle in his body tense.

"Would you please sit?" She sounded almost like she was begging.

Adrian relaxed, but only a little. He took a seat in the chair by the bed, completely unsure of himself in this situation.

"Heavens, this is terribly awkward, isn't it? Perhaps you could tell me a joke?"

"A joke?"

"Yes, something amusing. Laughter is good medicine for awkward moments."

Adrian was able to admire her tousled blonde hair, a rich honey gold, as she sat up. Whoever had the good fortune to marry this woman would be gifted with such a sight every day. A flash of sudden and almost violent jealousy filled him toward this husband who did not yet even exist.

"I'm afraid I don't know any jokes," he replied. "I'm a rather serious type."

"Oh dear, I see that you are." She giggled, and the delightful sound made him smile. "There. You can smile at least. My maid, Phoebe, says you are like Lord Byron. I rather agree."

"Should I be complimented or insulted by the comparison?"

"I'm sure Phoebe meant it as an insult. But from me, it is a compliment to be sure."

Adrian relaxed a little more. Conversation with the lady was not as hard as he'd imagined. With the other servants, conversation was easy. They all had the same sort of lives: endless work, the need to be quiet, respectful, and, as much as they could, invisible. But a lady like Venetia was born to be on display.

Her every look, action, and piece of clothing was a carefully constructed visual statement.

He could not help but continue the mental comparison between them. He lived in the basement of a grand country house, held only a few personal possessions to his name, and his life was dedicated to the comfort and pleasure of others. But her life was a happy balance of country leisure and the cultivation of her mind. The house she lived in would be filled with fine furniture and lovely portraits, her library would be well stocked, and classical sculptures no doubt graced the corridors of her townhouse. Her life was enviable.

"If we have no jokes to tell, perhaps we could become better acquainted?" Venetia suggested. "Would you tell me about yourself?"

"What do you wish to know?" He did not see this line of inquiry lasting very long. His life was completely uninteresting.

"Oh, start at the beginning, as all good stories must." Her tone was teasing, but it was sweet rather than cruel.

"The beginning?" Adrian leaned back, rubbing his shoulders against the soft cushions of the wingback chair, and he stroked his chin as though deep in thought. This earned another giggle from his fair charge.

"I was born in Northumberland, in a town called Blanchard."

"Oh, I believe I have heard of it. That is south of Hexam, is it not?"

"Yes, about nine miles. Are you familiar with the town?"

"No, not really, only that it is close to Hexam."

"Very well, then—I shall treat you to a history of the town."

She grew quiet, and he chuckled, sensing her disappointment. "I promise to make it mildly interesting."

"Only mildly? Dear me." She was smiling again. Lord, he adored her smile. It made him feel like he was out in the gardens on a spring day, the sun warming his face.

"Minx," he teased, then stopped short. He had crossed a line. That was an endearment meant for a teasing town wench. She chucked a pillow at him, and he caught it, grinning again.

"Well, go on," she urged, not at all bothered by him calling her a minx.

"Right," he said, clearing his throat. "Blanchard is a rather neatly arranged town. It's square, like the barracks of a foreign army instead of a meandering set of streets. The cottages are all made of gray and yellow stone, and they form disciplined lines around the village square, which is shaped a bit like the letter

L. Most of the townsfolk are miners and their families."

"Miners? Like for silver?" Venetia's eyes widened with curiosity.

"Nothing so romantic as that. They mine for lead. Most of the houses were built a century ago, and the village itself is very old. Twelfth century, in fact. The village square used to be the location of an old abbey."

"The abbey isn't there now?"

"No, sadly not. You see, Blanchard lies deep in a valley near the river Derwent, surrounded by bleak moorlands. Local legends say the seclusion of these moors prompted the Scots to visit during their raids across the border in 1327."

Venetia's eyes brightened. "Now we are discovering some intrigue. What happened in 1327?"

"Well, the monks were so relieved to have been delivered from those brutal Highland raiders that they rang the abbey bells in celebration, but the bells tolled so loudly in the valley that the Scots heard, turned around, and came back, sacking the abbey."

"How dreadful!"

"It is, rather. We do not even know what the abbey looked like. Only rubble was left after the raiders left, and eventually that was used for other structures, until the foundation was the only thing left. It now makes up Blanchard's village square. But

Blanchard was not yet done with the Scots or their legends." Adrian had to admit he was rather enjoying this discussion. He tossed the pillow playfully back at Venetia. She ducked with a giggle.

"More Scots? Pray, tell me."

"Blanchard was the home, at least for a time, of General Benjamin Forster, who led an unsuccessful Jacobite uprising in 1715. He escaped after he was captured at Preston, and he hid in Blanchard in a priest hole behind the fireplace in his home. The hole is still there today. And some say that Forster's sister, Dorothy, haunts the area around the fireplace."

"A ghost?"

"Yes. She is said to appear to visitors, asking them to take a message to Benjamin, who fled to France."

"What message?"

"I don't believe anyone knows. I believe most who have seen her simply run away before she can elaborate."

Venetia laughed. "I suppose I would run away too. One never knows what a ghost intends. Some can be pleasant, others quite frightening."

Adrian leaned forward and propped his arms on his knees. "You've seen a ghost?"

"Oh yes. At our old country house in the Lake District. We lived in Wetheral, in Cumbria."

"You don't live there any longer?"

Her happiness began to melt away. "No, we don't.

My father, the late Earl of Latham, passed away last year. My cousin is now Lord Latham, and he sold our country estate, Latham House. We were forced to live with him in our London townhouse."

"Why? Were you in need of money?" He realized too late that the question was inappropriate. "I'm sorry, please do not answer that."

"No, I don't mind," she assured him. "I have no need of money, but my cousin is . . . well, Gran calls him a wastrel. He prefers games of chance to other pastimes and came into the earldom with a large number of debts. The sale of the Latham country house paid them off, and he lined his pockets very well, but . . ." Her tone softened as her voice trailed off.

"But it cost you your home."

She sighed and wiped the sadness from her expression with false cheeriness. "That house had a fair number of ghosts, like the shrieking bride."

"The shrieking bride?" Adrian chuckled.

"Oh yes. And she did shriek too. She would chase you down the long picture gallery, wailing something dreadful, her eyes glowing red. I was very scared of her as a child. One night she chased me, and I don't know why but I turned about and shouted at her to be quiet. She simply vanished, and I have not seen her since."

"A sensible ghost! How thoughtful."

This time Venetia's answering smile was genuine, not forced. "But you distracted me. Tell me about you, please."

"I have not lived a life worth discussing, I fear."

"I don't believe that. All lives hold something of interest in them."

He glanced her way, saw her determined curiosity. He could not avoid the discussion, which only served to irritate him. "My mother was unwed, and my birth was of a scandalous nature. There, does that prove interesting enough?"

He didn't mean for his words to come out so harshly, but they did. There was so much inside him that still churned with anger and pain at what his father had done to his mother and to him.

Venetia's gaze was so beautiful and yet so solemn. "Your birth is not your fault, and I'm sure it isn't *that* scandalous."

Her attempt to placate him only irritated him further. How could she understand what he was trying to tell her?

"My lady, I am the bastard son of a duke who refuses to claim me. That is the definition of scandalous."

Venetia tilted her head, studying him. He didn't like to be the object of her scrutiny, at least not in this fashion.

"I'm deeply sorry for teasing you. I cannot

imagine the anxiety that must create. Would you forgive me?"

Adrian stared at the floor, trying to burn holes in the oriental carpets. "I should not have lost my temper, my lady. It is I who should be begging forgiveness from you."

"Not at all. You are entitled to your anger. I am the one who is sorry. Come, let us be friends again."

He stared at the small elegant hand she offered. "I . . ."

"Please?"

He could not deny those dark eyes anything. He stood and took her hand in his, shaking it gently in new friendship. Then he remembered that he had brought food.

"I've completely forgotten your lunch." He nodded toward the tray when Venetia did not release his hand immediately. He pulled away from her, slowly, their fingertips lingering together.

"I suppose I am a little hungry. Will you join me?" She sat up in bed as he brought the tray to her and laid it down on the blue satin counterpane.

"I shouldn't, my lady."

"Venetia, please. I must insist."

"Venetia." Adrian caressed her name as he spoke it.

"See? That wasn't hard, was it?" she teased him again. "Now, eat, please, or I will feel rude. If my grandmother wishes for you to be a companion and not a servant, then I will treat you as a companion, which means you will eat with me."

Seeing as he could not argue, Adrian stole one of the smaller plates from the tray and took a bit of food for himself.

"I am trying to find something terribly embarrassing to tell you about me, something that would put us on even ground." Venetia bit into a strawberry as she said this, and Adrian was drawn to the sight of her luscious lips.

"You do not need to put us on even ground. It was my mistake to burden you with the nature of my birth."

"I have it!" she exclaimed, her eyes alight with mischief. "My dreadful secret is that I am four and twenty and have yet to be kissed."

Adrian nearly dropped his plate onto the floor.

"Dreadful, isn't it? My first two seasons were quite disappointing. My father had so convinced me that dancing, balls, and all the things other girls dream of weren't important. He wanted me to be educated, to be focused on understanding our country estate, the wealth he'd invested and how best to manage it. After that, balls seemed so silly. My father allowed me to attend only a handful of dances, where the ladies always outnumbered the men. It was rather distressing to wait forever to be asked onto the floor by a gentle-man. And since I am not the prettiest of the ladies, I was overlooked when it came to amorous adventures."

"You're teasing," Adrian said. "You must've had at least a dozen men mad for you and at least a dozen kisses stolen."

She chuckled at his expression, which he knew must have looked quite stunned.

"It's true! I swear it. By my third season, well, I'm sure you know how much a man makes of a woman who is firmly on the shelf. I was entirely uninter-esting by then, even to the fortune hunters. My father appeared to be in good health, and before his death my dowry was considerable, though not overly attractive. Now I have inherited most of his money, and my wretched cousin Patrick inherited only the title. He thinks he can marry me off to some awful man of his choosing who will give him part of my inheritance."

Adrian stared at her. "That is why your grand-mother wishes you married?"

"Yes, exactly. But I want to choose who I marry. Not be forced into it by my scheming cousin or my well-meaning grandmother. Yet I am running short on time." She sighed and pushed away her tray on the bed. "I simply don't know the first thing about men." She was quiet a long moment, and then her gaze slid to him, a gleam in her dark eyes. "Adrian, would you teach me?"

"Teach you?"

"Yes. Teach me about men."

For the second time in her presence, Adrian choked and had to retrieve a cup of tea, only to trip and fall to the floor.

"I need to know about men. Their habits, their desires, courtship, attraction—even about kisses."

❦ 5 ❦

Venetia's heart raced as she watched the dashing footman recover himself. She thought she had nearly killed him as he choked and tripped trying to reach the tea tray nearby. She giggled as he regained his control. She hadn't meant to catch him off guard like that.

"Well? Will you teach me? I am sure I can compensate you in some way . . . If you would tell me what you might wish for. Consider yourself a tutor, and I your willing pupil."

Adrian now stood by the window, leaning against the frame, arms crossed, his gaze turned upon the gardens below. The silence between them was heavy, and Venetia turned her focus to the lean, trim lines of his body, which looked so dashing in the black-and-gold livery. He inspired such a dangerous longing within her for things she'd never felt before.

"Even if I wished to accept such an offer, it is out of the question. I would lose my position here for fraternizing with one of the guests." She swore she heard regret in his voice, as though he wished he could tutor her and that only their social standing prevented it.

Venetia had expected that response, but she hadn't expected to feel so disappointed by it. Although that hardly seemed a strong enough word for what she felt.

"Adrian, no one would know. You see how easily I sent Phoebe away. There is no one here to witness anything we speak of or do."

He faced her then, a wild look in his amber eyes as he stalked toward the bed. He braced one hand above her head on the headboard and leaned down.

"What you ask of me is dangerous. I am a passionate man, a man who enjoys the company of women, and if you let me have a single kiss, I'll want more. Neither of us can allow that."

Venetia swallowed, her eyes wide as she stared at that sensual mouth of his, which was still handsome even when turned down in a fierce scowl.

"Please, I can trust no one else with this. But I trust you."

"How can you trust me? You do not know me," he growled. "What if I was some wild libertine?"

"Are you?"

"No, but . . . bloody hell, woman." He leaned down with his free hand and cupped her chin. In a blinding flash, his mouth covered hers. Venetia whimpered at the hot touch of his lips against hers. She parted her lips in a gasp, and his tongue slid into her mouth. A bolt of heat shot through her, and the excitement she felt was almost unbearable. Never in her life had she felt like this. Never. It was frightening and exciting and confusing.

Adrian groaned as his hand moved from her chin to cradle the back of her head. She reached up to catch his cravat and curled her fingers in the cloth. The need to touch him, to be closer in any way she could, was overpowering. His mouth was as ravenous as hers. These wild new sensations caused by that single kiss left her reeling and dizzy. If she hadn't had hold of his neckcloth, she might have swayed.

His taste was delicious, with a hint of fruit and tea, and the feel of his tongue playing with her own was erotic in a way she never could have imagined. Venetia tried to wrestle her body free of the blankets to better touch him, to better press herself against him, but her ankle twinged and she pulled back from him to gasp in pain.

Their faces were still close, their breaths hard and

eyes half-closed. Adrian's hand was still tangled in her hair, and he gently massaged her scalp while she held his neckcloth. For a minute they simply stared into each other's eyes, both undone by that kiss.

Venetia didn't want to break the spell of that moment, but like all good things, it was certain to end. Adrian straightened and released her, his fingers threading through the strands of her hair as he pulled them free.

"I . . ." Again he was speechless, and this time so was she. Her first kiss. What a wonderous thing it had turned out to be.

"I'm very sorry," Adrian finally said. "I shouldn't have—"

"I wanted you to, and I thank you for it." She needed him to understand the gift he had given her. That kiss had been one born of desire and not out of an intent to court her for her money. It had been a true kiss, and no matter what happened later, who she married and settled upon, this kiss would always be special. She vowed to tuck this moment away in her heart and cherish it.

Adrian paced along the foot of her bed and scowled as he dragged his fingers through his hair. "I should not have done that."

"Did you not enjoy it?" Venetia asked, trying not to sound worried.

"Of course I did. That isn't the point. You are a

lady, and I am . . . no one." He turned to face her. "I will speak to Lady Devon. This arrangement will not work." He started toward the door, but Venetia threw back the covers and tried to get out of bed. In her desperation to stop him, she forgot her ankle. The moment she put weight on it, she cried out and fell.

Adrian was there, catching her in his arms. She could feel the strength of his body as he held her, and it sent a thrill through her.

"I swear, before I met you, I was not so clumsy or so foolish," Venetia said as she leaned gratefully against him.

A deep, amused chuckle rumbled through his chest, vibrating against her in a most wonderful way. "I don't normally choke, but it seems you deprive me of air."

She laughed and then let out a weary sigh.

"Tired?" he asked.

The gentle tone was back in his voice, one of concern and compassion. She wasn't used to it—not from a man, at any rate.

"A little. You must think me very frail and delicate, but I swear to you I am a much hardier creature."

"You've suffered an injury, and you were out for a long walk in the cold rain. That would make anyone tired."

He lifted her up and placed her back on the bed.

She caught his hand and held on to him before he could pull away.

"Please, do not speak to Lady Devon. You have been so wonderful, and I do wish to have you as a companion. If I promise not to ask for any more kisses, will you stay?"

Adrian looked at her for a long moment, and she could not read his expression.

"No more kisses. I can't afford to lose my position. Due to my birth and my age, it would be difficult to find work elsewhere."

"I understand." And Venetia did. The last thing she wanted was for him to risk his livelihood to satisfy her curiosity, but she couldn't get his kiss out of her mind, how it had made her feel so alive.

"Why don't you sleep? I need to report downstairs and attend to some tasks. I will return in a few hours."

"Thank you, Adrian."

She released his hand, and he bowed as he exited the room. Venetia was tired, but as she lay back in bed and closed her eyes, she could only think about that magnificent kiss.

ADRIAN WAS PLAYING WITH FIRE. A FIRE THAT burned so sweetly, he would enjoy every minute as it burned his world down around him. Adrian lingered in the corridor for a long moment as he fixed his neckcloth and desperately searched for the vanishing threads of his sanity.

Lady Venetia wanted him to teach her about men, about desire and attraction. He wasn't sure that such things could be taught. He'd heard braggarts in town boast of their dubious conquests, and he'd seen the quietest of men manage to win the affections of unattainable women. There were no set laws in the ancient art of courtship, yet he had foolishly agreed to educate her about it.

This would certainly get him tossed out of Hartland. The question was, how long would it be before he was discovered? He made barely thirty pounds a year, and it was not likely he would find such a position again. He would be forced into learning a new trade, assuming anyone would take him in. Life in service had prepared him only for other positions in service. He knew nothing of blacksmithing or mining. He could ride quite well, but he had no groom's experience that would make him indispensable to a new household. By agreeing to Lady Venetia's bargain, he was condemning himself.

Adrian managed to slip down to his room in the basement without being bothered by anyone. He sat down on his cot and buried his face in his hands. Ten years—for *ten years* this had been his home, the closest he'd come to a family after his mother had died. Adrian let out a heavy sigh. A sampler hung on the wall, words of wisdom sewn into the fabric with delicate precision: "Humility is a servant's true dignity."

He had plenty of humility. Losing his mother, then reaching out to his father only to be cast aside without so much as an audience. His mother had been certain Lord Stratford would agree to see him. It was a blessing she had not lived to know otherwise.

Yes, Adrian had plenty of humility and even more humiliation. But when he'd kissed Lady Venetia, there had been a brief moment where he had not felt like himself. No, that wasn't right. He'd felt more like himself than he had since he'd come to Hartland. He hadn't been an invisible servant, nor had he been a peacock to be put on display for his attractiveness. He'd simply been a man kissing a woman with passion and longing.

No doubt he was but a plaything to her, a toy to entertain and amuse. Then again, he had seen such sweet innocence in her eyes, as though he had kissed a princess awakened from a century-long slumber, rather than a scheming woman who wished to amuse herself with him. What was the truth? The princess or the clever creature who saw him as a toy? He had fended off advances from beautiful women who had stayed under this roof before. Turning them down had been easy. But Lady Venetia? She was different. And dangerous.

The dinner bell rang outside. He stood and hastily fixed his jacket and hair before he joined the others for their late midday meal. By the time he reached the servants' table, Mr. Reeves was already presiding at one end and the young housekeeper, Mrs. Miller, at the other.

Adrian slipped into his seat, head down, and Mr. Reeves recited a brief grace. After that, everyone sat in their assigned seats. Mrs. Webster passed plates full of shepherd's pie around the table.

"The guests have all arrived," Mr. Reeves began. "The maids and valets will be dining with us after the guests have eaten their supper this evening." Mr. Reeves spoke more about the fine lords and ladies who had arrived, but Adrian wasn't listening. He lifted his head only once while eating, and he saw Phillip watching him curiously.

When the meal was over, Adrian joined Benjamin to carry up trays of afternoon tea to the ladies, but Phillip caught up with him. Adrian nodded at Benjamin to go on ahead while he and Phillip hung back.

"Mr. Reeves said you have special duties this week. Is everything all right?" the valet asked.

"Yes, but I can't speak about it."

"It has to do with Lady Venetia, doesn't it?"

"Yes."

Phillip chuckled. "Well now, you've pleased the lady, then, by rescuing her. Well done, old boy!"

"Don't congratulate me. I may be in trouble still," Adrian replied before he followed Benjamin up to the green drawing room.

The ladies were all seated about the fire, whispering and laughing as Adrian and Benjamin set down the tea trays. The duchess preferred the footmen to serve the tea while she was engaged in conversation with her guests. Benjamin and Adrian moved efficiently through the room before they retreated into the hall to be silent sentries. Lady Devon was farther away from them, but a few of the other ladies were closer to their position. It was hard not to overhear some of what they said.

"She always has the most attractive men, don't you agree?" one woman asked another. Their gazes turned to Adrian and Benjamin, who stood in view from the doorway.

"She certainly does. If my husband weren't here . . . ," one mused, and her companion giggled.

Adrian clenched his jaw, and Benjamin shifted slightly on his feet. There was nothing more humiliating than being talked about as a commodity to be owned and coveted. He tried to ignore the ladies' conversation until Lady Venetia's name pulled him out of his thoughts.

"I hear Lady Latham's granddaughter is here," said the first woman. "Yes, the heiress. It's rumored she may finally be husband hunting, but the poor thing has twisted her ankle. Pity, that. My brother is here, you know, and I hope to set him in her path. He is in need of a wife with deep pockets."

"Oh? What if he brought her some flowers or some other token of interest? I daresay she would see it as very romantic, and he would have a chance to catch her attention without the other gentlemen around."

"That is an excellent idea. I shall tell Peregrine that. I'm sure that Lady Devon would part with some roses—she has so many in the hothouse."

An idea came to Adrian at the lady's suggestion. It filled him with a silly hope that he could do something to please Lady Venetia the way a proper gentleman would. He knew he shouldn't leave his post, but if he was smart about it, he could leave Benjamin in charge for a short while.

Adrian glanced at Benjamin. "I need to see to Lady Venetia. You have it handled here?"

Benjamin nodded. "Go on, I'll be fine."

"Thank you." Adrian slipped out of the corridor, emboldened with an idea. He wanted to bring Lady Venetia flowers, but real ones, not ones grown in the hothouse. He had an hour before he needed to return to her, so he went into the gardens and took his time speaking with the gardener, Mr. Paisley, who helped him cut several of the finest rose blooms and dozens of wildflowers. Adrian brought the bouquet inside the servants' hall and headed to the housekeeper's parlor.

Mrs. Miller was reviewing account books as he entered. The housekeeper, formerly Lady Devon's maid, had taken over after the previous housekeeper had departed. She was close to his own age. She was smart and capable as well.

"Are those for me?" Mrs. Miller teased when she saw the bouquet.

"I . . . No, but I was hoping to enlist your help. Would you happen to have a bit of ribbon or fabric to bind the stems together?" Adrian inquired.

"I might." She rose from her desk and went to a chest of drawers, pulling the top one open. It was full of odds and ends, with plenty of ribbon. She selected one that was a deep red, which matched the fattest rose blooms, and bound the bouquet up for him. Adrian felt wildly boyish with excitement.

"Let me guess. These are for Lady Venetia?" Mrs. Miller asked.

"Yes. I suppose everyone belowstairs must know of my temporary assignment by now."

Mrs. Miller laughed. "Nothing stays a secret long belowstairs."

"Thank you for the ribbon. You shall be remembered in song and story through the ages." He smiled at the young housekeeper, and she shoved him out of her office with a laugh.

Adrian returned to Lady Venetia's room, his heart filled with a strange, fluttering excitement. He halted at her door, which was partially open, and heard a man's voice from within.

". . . heard that you were poorly, Lady Venetia. I brought a gift for you."

"Oh my. These are very lovely flowers, Mr. Sherman. I shall send my maid out for a vase in a moment."

"You are most welcome, Lady Venetia. I thought you might be missing the gardens while you are confined up here."

"I am indeed."

"I also thought you might enjoy this." Mr. Sherman offered Lady Venetia a small velvet box. She opened it, and her eyes widened at whatever lay inside before she lifted her gaze to the gentleman.

"Oh, it is too precious," Lady Venetia gasped. "I cannot . . ."

"Please, I insist. It is a gift for you since you have brightened this party for me immensely."

Whatever Mr. Sherman had brought her must be exquisite and expensive—far above anything Adrian could ever give her.

Adrian's heart sank. The flowers slipped from his

fingers to the floor. He turned away and retreated back to the domain he'd been born into. The place where he would always belong.

I was a fool to think . . . A fool to dream.

Venetia did her best to have an interesting conversation with Mr. Sherman, one of the gentlemen attending the house party. The bouquet of flowers from Lady Devon's hothouse now sat in a vase on the table between them.

"Dreadful thing to turn one's ankle," Mr. Sherman said. "Done it myself as a lad." His eyes, a warm brown, were friendly enough, and his face was kind. He was one and thirty, with a decent estate attached to his name. He was polite, kind, seemed to value her thoughts and opinions, and was very attractive. Mr. Sherman was a man worth marrying, but the fire she'd experienced with Adrian simply wasn't there.

"If you feel up to it, I would like to sit with you in the gardens or on the back terrace later," Mr. Sherman said hopefully.

"Thank you. I would enjoy that."

"Well, I should leave you to rest." He bashfully smiled as he rose from his chair and took his leave. Phoebe sat in a corner, tending to a tear in Venetia's blue gown.

"He seems nice, my lady."

"He is, isn't he?" She held back how she truly felt, however. "Phoebe, could you have Adrian bring up some tea?"

"Of course." Phoebe set the sewing aside and left, only to halt outside the door and bend down. She picked up something that lay by the door.

"My lady?" Phoebe said uncertainly as she carried in the most exquisite bouquet of flowers Venetia had ever seen. It put Mr. Sherman's carefully raised hothouse flowers to shame.

"Oh my. Where did these come from?" She held out her hands, and Phoebe placed the bouquet in her arms. Venetia buried her face in the blooms. Red roses were tucked in the bouquet, along with dozens of stunning wildflowers. Pale-yellow primroses blended with bluebells, marigolds, scarlet pimpernels, and the brightly colored stems of pink lady's-gloves. Their floral scent still held a touch of storms about them. These had come from the gardens in the field. A red satin ribbon was carefully tied around the stems, holding them together.

"They were on the floor, as if someone dropped them." Phoebe stared at the flowers, a curious expression on her face.

"Could you find another vase for these?" Venetia asked. She felt a strange pull toward the wild blooms, as though if she let go of them she would lose something precious to her. She could not express this feeling in words, so until a vase could be found, she would hold on to them.

"I shall run down to the kitchens and have the footman bring your tea while I find another vase."

"Thank you, Phoebe." Venetia rose from her chair and winced as she hobbled over to the table and moved Mr. Sherman's vase to the windowsill. She'd insisted that Mr. Sherman not give her the necklace that he'd brought. It was far too precious an item for her when she barely knew him. It was more suited for the announcement of an engagement, which neither of them had discussed. He'd wanted her to keep the jewelry, but she'd told him that the flowers were far more to her taste in gifts, and thankfully he hadn't seemed upset by it. Mr. Sherman was quite a kind man. If only she felt about him the way she felt about Adrian, her future would be so clear.

Venetia sat back down in her chair, her hands still wrapped around the blooms. She breathed in the scent again and smiled as they made her think of Adrian. She had many more questions to ask him about men now that she'd had a chance to compare him to Mr. Sherman. Such as why he made her feel wild, lost, and breathless with excitement when Mr. Sherman did not. That was a most important question indeed.

$\mathcal{H}$ 6 $\mathcal{H}$

"She's asking for you," Phoebe announced as she entered the servants' dining room.

Adrian glanced up from polishing a silver teapot. "I must finish this first," he replied quietly. He didn't want to go up there and see her being courted by that gentleman. Nor did he want to see the flowers he'd spent so long picking and then foolishly abandoned on the floor like a sulking child. His actions made him feel like a coward, but he couldn't go back up there and see her beaming from another man's attentions, not when he'd held such a foolish hope that she might . . . Adrian banished the thought.

Phoebe stood in front of him, her stern expression softening. "She prefers yours."

"Pardon?" Adrian focused back on the teapot,

rubbing over-vigorously on a stubborn spot of tarnish.

"Your flowers. The ones I found outside my mistress's room. I didn't tell her they were yours, but she took to them right away, more so than Mr. Sherman's."

Adrian stilled. "She liked them?"

"She did, buried her face right in them and smiled. She sent me to fetch you for tea while I find another vase."

Adrian's smile faded a bit. "I need to finish this or Mr. Reeves will have my head."

"Take it upstairs and work on it. Lady Venetia won't mind."

"Won't mind watching a man earn his living?" Adrian grumbled. He was not normally a man to indulge in self-pity, but he couldn't seem to stomach the thought of Venetia seeing him perform the common duties of a footman.

Phoebe crossed her arms in a severe fashion. "My lady fancies you, and I would hate to see her disappointed."

Adrian pushed his chair back and sighed. "Very well. I will be up shortly with her tea."

"Good." The lady's maid left the servants' hall, and Adrian caught Benjamin's arm as he passed by.

"If you see Mr. Reeves, tell him I've been

requested to see to Lady Venetia, and I have taken the teapot with me.

"I will let him know," Benjamin promised.

Adrian prepared a tea tray, collected his pot and polishing cloth, and made the climb up to Lady Venetia's bedchamber. He hesitated before knocking, and then he pushed the door open when she called for him to enter. She was seated by the fire, wearing a lovely day gown of a soft lilac with a dark-purple sash around her waist. Her face was less pale, and her brown eyes glowed with delight as he came inside. His flowers were resting in a vase beside her on the table, the other flowers now tucked away on the windowsill.

She beamed at him. "I'm glad you're back, Adrian. I've created a list of questions for you to answer." She glanced around and then leaned toward him as he drew near. "And I've sent Phoebe on a few errands, so we shan't be disturbed."

"Oh dear. Now you have me worried," Adrian said with a chuckle. "Dare I listen to these questions?"

"You must. Now sit," she commanded, though her tone was teasing rather than imperious. He sat down across from her in a companion chair.

"Very well, ask your questions."

"I wish to know more about what men desire in a woman. Do you worry about looks or her mind more? My father always warned me that most men prefer looks, but I believe he was rather biased in trying to keep me from wanting to marry. Would you say it depends on the man?"

"Well, you've jumped right into the thick of it, haven't you?" He laughed but then turned serious. "It definitely depends on the man. A *good* man wants a woman to have a strong mind and a brave heart. Beauty shines from within, and the brighter that inner shine, the greater the outer shine becomes. A pretty face fades. As men and women grow older together, it's what's inside that matters."

"I agree," Lady Venetia replied. She twined her fingers in her skirts, then reached for the bouquet of flowers he'd brought. Her fingers brushed over the blooms of a few bluebells. He sucked in a breath when he noticed how lovingly she was gazing upon the flowers he'd chosen for her.

"Adrian, did you . . . ? Are these yours?"

He hadn't expected this change of subject.

"Er . . . Yes. I picked those for you." His voice was a little rough, so he cleared his throat.

"Why didn't you bring them to me? Phoebe found them on the floor in the corridor."

Adrian looked away. "I saw Mr. Sherman here, paying court to you, and his flowers were . . ." He paused, searching for the right words. "Mine seemed inadequate."

"Mr. Sherman's flowers are delicate selections

from Lady Devon's hothouse, and I doubt he chose them himself. They are lovely, but these . . ." She smiled at his bouquet. "These are flowers that lived out in the wide world, beautiful and bold, wild and free, even the garden roses. They have earned their place in the world. They are not pampered plants who have water and soil given to them at their leisure."

Adrian was silent. Her words moved him deeply, and she fell quiet too for a long moment.

"Mr. Sherman's flowers are a kind gesture. Yours, however, are a statement. Thank you. They brightened my dreary day."

Her words sent a flutter of hope through him again, but he knew better than to embrace it. Still . . . she had surprised him with her view on the flowers.

"You're welcome, my lady. I was asked to teach you about men, but it seems instead you have taught me something about women."

She smiled then as she looked his way. "Now, we shall return to my questions. The next one is that I wish to know more about you."

"Me? My lady, we have been over this." He shook his head. "I am supposed to talk to you about men, not me."

"You are a man, aren't you?" She hid all the humor from her face as she gave him a guileless, innocent look.

"I am," he reluctantly agreed.

"Good. Now, tell me about your mother."

"My mother?"

"Yes." Lady Venetia sat there, prim and proper, and all Adrian could think was that she needed some good and proper kissing to distract her. At the risk of losing his position, he took a chance.

"My lady, why don't we return to the subject of desire?"

An excited heat lit her eyes. "Desire?"

"Yes. Desire, while not necessary for marriage, is important for a happy one."

She leaned forward, eager to hear more. "Do go on."

Adrian stood and began to pace the room. "Desire can begin with a look." He paused and turned toward her, allowing every wicked thought he'd ever had about her to break through his reserved exterior. He thought of the way her satin-smooth skin had felt as he had helped undress her. He thought of what he would do to her if he were of her station, how he would catch her in some private alcove, hike up her skirts, and claim her, overwhelming her with pleasure.

Her face flushed red, and her lips parted. With a single look, he had proved that desire could be seen in a man's eyes.

"I . . ." She swallowed hard. "I meant to say, what

else do you know about desire? Can it develop over time if it does not come instantly?"

"It can. Just like love, desire can grow over time, but it can also fade over time. Do not marry a man simply out of desire. Marry him for love too." He paused, thinking over his own choices regarding marriage. He'd never felt a deep devotion to any woman before. *Desire*, yes, but never *love*. The truth was, he'd never dared give in to thoughts of love and marriage. It wasn't his destiny as a person in service.

"I know, love is very important. But I worry . . ." She trailed off, her eyes drifting to something beyond him.

He came back and sat again in the chair nearest her. "About what?"

"I worry that I will not be able to find a man who will love me." He saw the flash of trepidation mixed with hope in her eyes as she spoke. "I am not meek, nor biddable. I do not have the least bit of interest in obeying a man simply because he commands me to. I certainly don't believe men are superior—if they were, they would be the ones trusted to bear children and raise them. That duty is reserved to us ladies, yet we are treated so abominably."

She spoke with such forlorn sorrow that Adrian was moved to act. He reached across the space between them and took hold of one of her hands. "Did your father treat you poorly?"

"Oh no, quite the opposite. My mother died when I was thirteen, and he wanted me to be raised as a proud, intelligent, and independent woman. He cautioned me against the male sex so severely that until this business with my cousin trying to force me to marry his friend, I had no desire to marry at all."

"And now you are resigned to it?" he asked, trying to figure out the puzzle of Lady Venetia.

"Yes, I suppose that word fits as well as any." She looked into his eyes. "I want to be loved, desired, but also valued as a person, not seen as a bit of chattel that a man owns. I don't want to marry a man who just wants to obtain my fortune. Does such a man exist in England?"

Adrian still held her hand, and he slowly raised it to his lips. "Yes. There are good men who would desire, love, and cherish you the way you deserve." He wished more than anything to have been born a gentleman, not a bastard. To be a man worthy of her. He would have gladly given his soul away in a Faustian pact if he could have that one gift.

"Do you have a woman you love?" she asked as he lowered their joined hands back down.

"I am alone in the world. To marry would mean to leave Hartland Abbey, and while I have an excellent service record here, I cannot easily find work elsewhere. My parentage draws too much scandalous speculation, even after all these years."

"Is Lord Devon . . . ?"

"No, he's not my sire. He is kind and good. He took me in at my father's request. My father is the Duke of Stratford."

Lady Venetia's lips parted in shock. "Adrian, one of your half sisters is here for the house party."

Her excited whisper caused a spike of fear and confusion in him. "What? I saw no one from the house of Stratford on the guest list."

"She's Lady Mowbray, married to Viscount Mowbray. She can't be much older than you. How old are you?"

"I am nine and twenty," he replied, but his mind was now miles away. Had Mr. Reeves known that one of Adrian's half siblings was here? Surely he would have memorized the pedigree of each guest. Was that why he had allowed Adrian to stay away from the guests and tend to Lady Venetia instead?

"Oh, Adrian, what if you could meet her? She's very lovely. I've met her once or twice before at dinner parties in London. Her husband, Lord Mowbray, is charming and kind."

For a second he considered it, but then he laughed at his own foolishness. No matter how the little boy he'd once been who'd craved siblings wished for such an outcome, he could never let it happen. "No, I cannot meet her. She must never learn about me. I would lose my position here, and then I wouldn't be able to find other employment, because I have no other skills than service. I cannot afford to starve again."

With a little gasp, she covered her mouth with her hand. "Again?"

"I'm sorry, Lady Venetia. I have spoken out of turn. I should leave you to rest." He started to stand.

"Please don't. It seems I am constantly upsetting you with my careless conversation. Please do not leave. Please." She held out a hand to him.

For a long second, he battled within himself to do the right thing. To politely walk away. But damn her beautiful eyes, he could not leave.

He clasped her hand in his again, and the soft, relieved smile that curled her lips undid him. The loose gold waves of her hair tumbled down her shoulders, catching sunlight, which clung to it like a lover. She was exquisite. She was a goddess so far above his reach. Yet when she looked at him the way she was doing now, she felt more real to him than any woman he'd ever been with. Was it because he'd shared so much of himself with her? He'd never let himself be vulnerable like this with anyone.

"We won't speak of Lady Mowbray, I promise, but do you think you could arrange for us to have dinner in another room? My ankle feels less painful, and I would desperately like to be out of this blasted bedchamber. It doesn't suit me at all to feel like an invalid. I know I cannot attend dinner with the others, because that would require hobbling about quite foolishly, but surely we could have dinner outside of this room?"

Adrian tapped his chin. "I will speak with Mr. Reeves and see if we can have you dine in the upstairs library."

"Oh, lovely. I can't think of a better place."

Adrian collected the teapot from the tray and a cloth and sat down in a chair. He felt Lady Venetia's eyes on him, so he pretended to examine the teapot in his lap and began to rub a spot of tarnish, trying to ignore how self-conscious he felt in that moment.

"That must be very tedious. Shall I read to entertain you?"

"I . . . Yes, I'd like that very much."

Lady Venetia retrieved a book from a nearby table and began to read to him while he polished. For the first time in a long while, he lost himself in a story as he worked. Half an hour later, he was laughing with her as they discussed the Gothic romance she had been reading.

Lady Venetia wiped tears off her cheeks as she laughed so hard she cried. "You are right, these books . . . Oh, heavens . . ." She dissolved into giggles.

"I think it must be a requirement for the heroine of a Gothic novel to roam willy-nilly about in her thinnest nightgown and always carry a candelabra. It's a bloody miracle the castles aren't burned down, given all the flames waving wildly about."

"Oh, but I do like them," said Lady Venetia. "One always knows what to expect. The brutal hero who at last reveals his love and rescues the heroine from the true villain. There is some comfort in the predictability."

"Life is only interesting because it's unpredictable." Adrian set the now gleaming teapot on the tray just as Lady Venetia stood up.

"You think so?" she asked more quietly.

"Yes. There should be surprises in one's life. Predictability has its comforts, but no real excitement." He collected the tray and headed for the door. "I'll be back shortly to escort you to dinner in the upstairs library."

Lady Venetia smiled at him. "Thank you." Damned if his knees didn't buckle just a bit at that. It made her entire being simply glow.

Remember you are nothing to her, can never be anything to her.

And with that sobering thought, he descended belowstairs.

GWEN WAITED FOR THE HANDSOME FOOTMAN TO retreat with his tea tray before she stepped out of her hiding place. She had been delighted to hear Venetia's laughter and teasing with the young man as they enjoyed each other's company. Gwen had wanted to see how her granddaughter was faring and had hidden herself in the alcove next to a very grim marble bust of some Grecian fellow as she listened to Venetia and the servant.

This was what she'd hoped her dear Venetia would be experiencing: joy and delight with a man. The best husbands were the ones who could make their wives' hearts light with laughter. Marriages all had their challenges, but they should also bring joy to the couple.

Gwen paused at Venetia's partially open door and heard her granddaughter humming softly. For a moment, Gwen wondered if she had made a dangerous error in putting Venetia in the path of that attractive footman. What if she became attached?

No, it was all going to work out perfectly. Venetia would discover what mattered most in a husband, and she would follow her heart and find a worthy gentleman. And that sod Patrick could bloody well hang if he tried to interfere with Venetia's happiness again.

Tapping her knuckles on Venetia's door, Gwen called out, "It's me, my dear."

"Oh, Gran, come in," Venetia called.

Gwen pushed the door open and saw her granddaughter's glowing face. She looked much better after some rest and entertainment.

"How is your ankle?"

"Still swollen, but I have been rubbing it, which seems to relieve some of the tension. I can move about now. Not too fast, but if I need to, I am able." She wore a pair of fur-lined slippers and a lilac gown that favored her soft honey-gold hair. She looked enchanting. No wonder the poor footman had been in such good spirits, with this enchanting vision of Venetia here to make him smile.

"You seem in much better spirits," Gwen said.

"I am. Adrian is wonderful. He had to polish a teapot, so I read to him from *The Duke's Dark Son*, that Gothic novel I purchased last week."

"Did you say he polished a teapot? Please tell me he *actually* polished a teapot. I cannot deal with euphemisms for scandalous behavior today."

"Yes, it was an *actual* teapot. You didn't think we . . . ? Oh." She covered her mouth and almost laughed, but thought better of it.

"Good, I wouldn't want to think he was convincing you to tickle his piffle," Gwen muttered.

"Tickle his . . . piffle?" Venetia did laugh at this, and Gwen couldn't help but chuckle with her. "What, pray tell, is a piffle?"

"You know . . ." Gwen waved airily below her waist. "The male organ . . . as it were."

"Piffle," Venetia repeated, almost choking on her laughter. "Heavens! Gran, no wonder he chokes around you. Please never let him hear you call his . . . part . . . a piffle."

"Very well. I shall keep that to myself." Technically the word *piffle* meant nonsense, but she'd heard a man at a ball once mention the word in such a context, and it had delighted her ever since. It was a wonderfully apt description.

"Adrian is a good companion, and I like to hear his laugh. Such a lovely sound," Venetia confessed. "I don't think he laughs much. Not because he doesn't enjoy it, but because life in service must be very trying. I hadn't honestly given it much thought, but he must be very busy and lonely all at the same time. And it isn't fair because—" Venetia suddenly halted her speech.

Gwen fixed a sharp eye on Venetia. "What isn't fair?"

"I cannot say—it would be breaking his confidence."

"I see. Well, I hope he proves worthy of your secret keeping," Gwen replied. "You will be upstairs tonight for dinner?"

"I think so. It would be embarrassing to hobble about in front of all those prospective suitors."

"True enough. I heard Mr. Sherman paid his respects today."

"Oh, yes. He was most obliging."

"I hope it was a little bit more than that, my dear. He comes from a good family, and he's a decent sort. I knew his parents. Splendid folks."

"He is rather attractive," Venetia mused, but Gwen could see her thoughts were elsewhere.

"You could do worse than him for a husband."

"I could, but Gran, there is no fire, no heat."

Venetia blushed, and Gwen walked over and sat down beside her.

"And who is talking about fire and heat?"

"Oh, no one, but isn't that important?"

"Passion is important, but not everyone feels it right away. Passion can come over time."

"I know. If we only had time," Venetia grumbled.

Gwen felt awful for her beloved granddaughter being rushed in this monumental decision. "Yes, if only you did . . ."

※ 7 ※

Adrian was adjusting the time on the clock in the billiard room. It was one of Lord Devon's favorites, a French Louis XIV mantel clock made sometime in the 1660s. Mr. Reeves lectured all incoming footmen about the prestige and quality of the clocks and that it was their duty to keep them in pristine condition.

This clock was a delicate piece, with a case made of red tortoiseshell and ornamented with delicately cut inlays of copper and pewter. The case was accented with bronze mounts in the shapes of beadings, rosettes, palm leaves, fir cones, antique oil lamps, and claw feet. The clock's face was covered with black chamois leather.

Adrian carefully adjusted the ornate bronze clock

hands to the correct time based on the pocket watch in his waistcoat pocket. Beneath the circular display of roman numerals, a bronze figure of Chronos, the god of time, appeared to be holding up time itself. A heavy burden. Adrian could sympathize.

He had stepped back from the clock and turned toward the door when three of the gentlemen guests entered, one being Mr. Sherman. Adrian faded into the wall next to the marble mantel, doing his best to be unseen, yet not hiding, lest the gentlemen assume he was trying to eavesdrop.

"How did it go?" one of the men asked Sherman.

"Well enough. She, like all ladies, enjoys flowers," Sherman replied.

"Is it true that she is as rich as Croesus?" the second man asked.

"Not quite, but close," Sherman said. "Her cousin, Lord Latham, is desperate to marry her to one of his chums, no doubt with a cut of her fortune in mind as a repayment for his matchmaking efforts."

"Really?" The first man looked disgusted. "That man has the worst taste in friends."

"Indeed. He was speaking about it at Boodles. I wanted to throttle that man," Sherman growled. "It isn't done to speak of a woman in a club, especially not with such a mercenary intent."

"I would have backed you if you had throttled the

man, Sherman," the first man said, perhaps a bit boastfully.

Adrian watched in silence as the men set up a billiards game, oblivious to his presence for a moment, until Sherman addressed him.

"I say. Could you fetch us a bit of whiskey, if you don't mind? I know you must be tending to the clocks." Sherman, it was clear, had seen him setting the timepiece when he'd entered the room. He was an observant man—Adrian would have to remember that.

"Yes, sir." Adrian bowed and retreated, leaving the gentlemen alone as he fetched a drink cart from one of the salons. He rolled it back into the room and prepared three glasses, arranged them on a silver tray, and served them to the gentlemen as they continued to discuss Lady Venetia.

Sherman took a sip, nodded his thanks to Adrian, and turned back to the billiards game.

"If you truly mean to woo Lady Venetia, you had better act fast. I wouldn't put it past her cousin to try something fiendish and force a marriage on the poor woman," the second man said as he leaned on his pool cue.

"I agree. Latham would try something like that, the bounder, but for once, I wish to be decent about wife hunting," Sherman said. "I've been a bachelor for too long. A man cannot simply treat this like a tryst, not when he has marriage in mind. I mean to be faithful to whomever I marry and to make a match with a woman I love and respect. I don't wish to make a mistake, not in something this important."

"No, of course not," his friend agreed. "But you may need to help it along. Lady Venetia has no experience with men. At her age, she should have, but I've been told her father kept her very protected—the man only let her attend a handful of balls during her come-out. I suspect the poor girl has no idea of when she's being wooed. You might have to make your intentions more plain."

"Yes, I suppose I might. I believe she will miss dinner this evening, but I might pay a call afterward."

Adrian clenched his fists, hating Mr. Sherman, even though the man wasn't being ungentlemanly toward Lady Venetia. In fact, he seemed to be the sort of man she was looking for, one who thought of her mind and heart and wished to woo her with the best intentions. But the thought of another man touching her filled Adrian with jealous anger. An anger he knew full well that he had no right to feel.

"Just watch for that old dragon, Lady Latham," Sherman's friend warned in jest as he knocked back the rest of his whiskey. "She would have no qualms about walloping you over the head with that cane of hers if she thought you were being too forward." The gentlemen all chuckled at that.

The conversation soon turned to gambling, hunting, and other sports of leisure that Adrian had never had the means to indulge in. He saw that none of the men needed a second drink, so he hastily left. It was time to speak to Mr. Reeves about dinner. It would no doubt be an unpleasant discussion, but he would do anything for Lady Venetia now.

VENETIA FOUND HERSELF STRANGELY NERVOUS AS Phoebe finished styling her hair. She had changed for dinner, even though she was not going down with the other guests. She wore a deep-plum purple gown with a silver sash. Her hair was gathered in loose waves, and a ribbon had been threaded through her gold locks in a Grecian fashion.

"Would you say I look . . . attractive?" she asked the maid.

Phoebe arched a suspicious brow. "You have never asked me that before."

"Well, do I?"

"You look lovely, as always, my lady."

Venetia relaxed at her maid's sincere tone. "It is silly to be nervous, isn't it?"

"For dinner with a footman? I should certainly say so. *He* is the one who should be nervous."

"Oh hush." Venetia laughed at her maid's dour, disapproving *tut-tut* as she touched up a few stray curls.

"You look fit for the prince himself. If that footman knows what's good for him, he'll be stunned, my lady."

Venetia gazed at herself in the looking glass and for the first time did feel truly stunning.

"Do you wish me to help you to the upstairs library?"

"Oh, yes, please. I told Adrian I would meet him there. He still has so much to do."

Phoebe gently helped her stand, and Venetia took a few cautious steps on her still-tender foot. She was feeling much better but didn't want Adrian to know that. Her grandmother might force her back into the midst of the party, and she didn't want that, not when she could spend more time with him.

They walked to the upstairs library. Venetia's heart skipped a beat when she spied Adrian's form standing by the reading table. His head rose at the rustle of her dress, and he was soon at her side, bowing as he offered her his arm. Venetia saw the stern look that Phoebe gave to Adrian before she reluctantly set Venetia free.

A great sense of peace settled on Venetia as he

gently pulled her toward the reading table. Phoebe receded to the background; it was now just the two of them in the library.

"Tell me the truth. Was Mr. Reeves very mad at you?"

Adrian offered her a conspiratorial grin. "Mad enough. Lady Devon said I should do whatever I needed to please you, and I reminded him of that order, so he finally had to concede."

"Oh dear, I imagine a butler would not like that."

Adrian grinned. "No indeed. Mr. Reeves is a fair man, but the household has its rules, and he loves his rules. But he's been a good man to me." Adrian's expression darkened. "I came here half-starved, desperate, and he took me in, despite my history."

Venetia gave his arm a squeeze. "It's so unfair to judge a child for his birth. You would be a worthy heir to any dukedom, but I don't think I would've been a decent maid. Perhaps a housekeeper," she mused.

Adrian chuckled. "Housekeeping is a complicated position. It requires a lot of clever thinking and careful planning, as well as management of many different personalities. I have no doubt you would be excellent at it."

Venetia sat in the chair he pulled out for her. "What is life like downstairs? I am so rarely allowed downstairs, even in my own home."

He poured her a glass of wine and then one for himself. "It's busy at most times. Chaotic, even. We have very little time to be still. Someone is almost always underfoot or in your way. The kitchen is always hot, but it smells wonderful most of the time. Tonight it smells like nutmeg and roasted pheasant."

"That does sound rather lovely." Venetia sipped her wine. "Do you sleep upstairs or down?"

"Footmen sleep in the basement of the house, my lady. I share a room with another footman, Benjamin."

Venetia asked a dozen more questions about Adrian's life before she came back to the question that mattered most to her.

"Will you tell me about your mother?"

Adrian stared into the depths of his wine goblet, deep in thought.

"She was kind and beautiful. She was a country squire's daughter who became a governess when her family fell on hard times. She was hired by the Duke of Stratford to see to his two children."

"Your half sister and half brother, Viscount Bainbridge and Lady Mowbray?"

He paused a moment. "Yes. Their mother died a year after my mother came to work there. My mother said the duke was brokenhearted. He had been devoted to his duchess, but after her death he sought comfort in my mother's bed. When she learned she was with child, he sent her north. He gave us money every month, but I gained employment at sixteen to support her should the duke stop sending money. It was better that I should be able to support us both, but I only ever managed odd jobs or occasional work in a tavern. There were plenty of apprenticeships, but they wish for boys to start young, around thirteen, and those contracts bind you to your master in indentured servitude. I couldn't do that."

Venetia wanted to touch Adrian, to ease some of his pain, but she dared not show such compassion lest he mistake it for pity. Men had their pride, and she would not wound his.

"Your mother sounds wonderful."

"She was. She taught the local schoolchildren for eighteen years. She improved the lives of so many there." His smile was impossibly soft and sad all at once. It was clear that he had loved her deeply, but even the good memories brought him pain. "Even the local gentry sent their children to her. I sometimes think that, had she been a man, she would have been destined for something wonderful, a career as an engineer or an architect. Fate is cruel to brilliant women."

Venetia set her fork down as she looked at him. "You believe that women are capable of brilliance?"

"Capable? Certainly. If working downstairs has taught me anything, it's that women are just as strong, just as clever and hardworking, if not more so, than many men."

For a moment Venetia held her breath, suddenly unsure of herself.

"Adrian . . . if you were to marry, would you have an equal marriage?"

"An equal marriage?" Those amber eyes of his warmed her all over as she became the sole focus of his attention. "How do you mean?"

"How would you treat your wife?"

"With love and compassion, of course. But I expect you mean something more."

"What of matters of the home? Of finance or career?"

"She would certainly be consulted on any decision I made. I see marriage as a partnership, and for it to work well, it requires trust and communication from both parties."

"You would not subjugate her in any way?"

Adrian's eyes softened, and he leaned forward across the table toward her. "I've seen homes run that way before. It's as if the husband and wife live separate lives and are almost unaware of each other, merely residing in the same building. That is not a marriage I would care to have."

Venetia placed her palm in his, and he curled his fingers around hers. His thumb moved in a soothing pattern over her inner wrist, and her pulse pounded in excitement beneath that caress.

"I was raised by a strong, loving woman," Adrian continued. "The last thing I would do is crush a woman's spirit by not giving her the freedom she deserves. A man and wife should rely on each other, and not just for support. A marriage should be a partnership of equals." His voice was soft and held an unsung promise of what he would give the woman he would someday call his wife. It made Venetia's heart ache that she would not be that woman.

"That"—Venetia swallowed thickly—"is what I want in my marriage."

"Then we shall find it for you."

His promise created a wild stirring within her. They finished their wine and spoke of lighter subjects, with Adrian regaling her with humorous stories from downstairs. It was one of the most pleasant evenings she'd had in a long time. Adrian collected the dishes and set them on a tray, and it made her realize that in the last half hour she'd forgotten he was a footman. They had been simply two people engaging in a most absorbing discussion. Venetia got up and moved about the library, examining the towering shelves and reading the gilded titles on the spines.

Spying a collection of poems she recognized, she pulled the tome free from the shelf.

Adrian was close behind her, and the heat of his body against her back sent delicious shivers through her. She turned to face him, opening the book and holding it so that he could see only her eyes.

"Byron?" he chuckled. His lips slid into a lazy grin that made her knees weak.

"Fitting, I think," she replied, still using the book to shield her face. Adrian's eyes were warm with mischief as he placed one palm beside her head against the bookshelf and began to recite:

Fame, wisdom, love, and power were mine,
And health and youth possessed me;
My goblets blushed from every vine,
And lovely forms caressed me;
I sunned my heart in Beauty's eyes,
And felt my soul grow tender;
All earth can give, or mortal prize,
Was mine of regal splendor.

"You know your Byron," she teased. He slowly reached up and pulled the book away from her face, leaning close. She reveled in that moment when their faces almost touched, and she could see the glint of his eyes, the sensual quirk of his lips.

He stole a kiss. She moved toward him, needing to be closer. He cupped the back of her neck, his fingers holding her still as he deepened the kiss. She parted her lips eagerly for him, falling deeper into this wild, fluttering excitement that spread from her belly like a flock of butterflies taking flight.

"My God, you taste sweet," he groaned as he trapped her against the shelf.

She moaned as he began to slide a hand underneath her skirts, but the sudden sound of voices stopped them.

They froze. Adrian's hand still lay against her outer thigh, and her body trembled as they strained to better hear the approaching sounds. It was a pair of people, a man and a woman, who entered the library.

"This way. No one ever comes into a library." The man chuckled, and the woman giggled in response.

"Here," the woman said from close by. "Now, Monty, please. I need you." The woman sounded desperate and breathless.

"Of course, Lady Percy." Monty groaned, and there was the sound of clothing moving about, followed by another giggle from the woman.

Shocked by what they were about to hear, Venetia nearly gasped, but Adrian covered her mouth with his hand. Their eyes met, and he jerked his head toward the end of the bookcase, which had a patch of wall that was not lined with shelves. He waited to see if she understood.

She didn't know what he intended, but she nodded. Adrian dropped his hand from her mouth and took her hand in his, pulling her toward the gap. He traced the wall, feeling for something, and then he grinned and pressed his thumb into the wall. It gave way, opening up into a dark passageway. He pulled her into the darkness with him.

Venetia didn't speak as he closed the door behind them. They moved deeper into the tunnel, and shafts of light came through tiny pinpricks in the walls every now and then as they passed by other rooms. Venetia realized that these were tiny peepholes. Venetia and Adrian paused by one and took a moment to peer through it into a drawing room.

"Empty." Adrian started to push against the wall, but the sound of someone entering the room made him freeze again.

"I say, who's there?" a man demanded. He was a gray-haired gentleman, midsixties perhaps, and he carried a newspaper under his arm. He scanned the room with one eyebrow raised.

"Come out! I know you are here!"

Venetia held back a giggle, and Adrian covered her mouth again, his body pressed hard to hers in the narrow passageway. The giggle turned to a gasp as he raised her skirts. She threw her head back as his fingers explored the mass of her petticoats until he found the bare skin of her thigh above her stockings. He played with the ribbon of that stocking, and Venetia trembled with a wild, desperate hunger she had never felt before. She clutched at Adrian's shoulders, digging her nails into him to keep him close as he moved his hand through the frothy layers of her undergarments. Then he was touching her in that secret, sensitive place between her thighs. Adrian brushed his fingers through the thatch of curls over her mound and pressed one finger into her sex. She squeaked in surprise, unable to help herself.

"There it is again!" the man in the drawing room muttered. "Bloody mice in the walls. Wait until Lord Devon hears." The man's mutterings softened as he ambled away from the room, but Venetia was barely aware of him. All she could do was feel Adrian exploring her body. His other hand was still over her mouth to keep her quiet as he introduced her to a pleasure so exquisite that she nearly wept from the sudden rush of a climax that swept her away like a high tide.

Her legs buckled, and she would have collapsed if Adrian hadn't moved his hand from her mouth to hold her up. His fingers still thrust slowly in and out of her, drawing out the last little shocks of wonderment. Only then did he gently pull his hand out from under her skirts. In the dim light, she saw him slide his fingers between his lips and lick her essence clean.

She stared at him, her body quivering at his sensual wickedness.

She'd had no idea that a man could do anything like what Adrian had just done.

"You really are as wicked as Lord Byron," was all she could whisper.

He laughed, a deep, husky sound that held a delightful wickedness to it.

"I suppose I am, but I won't apologize. You are too tempting, my lady."

"I wouldn't dare ask you to, not when it was so wonderful." She moved sideways so she could better see his eyes.

He cupped her face and gazed down at her with soft, sweet eyes. "Was that your first release?"

"Heavens, it was a release, wasn't it? I thought for a moment I might die from it." She leaned into him as he curled his arms around her, embracing her.

"Thank you for giving me that gift," he whispered against her hair. There was such a reverence in his words that for a moment she felt like a goddess of old, bestowing gifts upon a mortal worshiper.

"You must be tired," he said after a few minutes. "Let me take you back to your room so you may rest your ankle."

Venetia wanted to protest, wanted to say she was his, but she was in fact quite tired.

"Will you come to my chamber tonight after everyone is asleep?" She needed him to be with her more than anything else.

"You wish me to?"

"Please. If you want to, that is. I don't wish to ask anything of you that you would not give freely, or if it might get you into trouble."

He was quiet a long moment and then nodded. "My wish is your wish. I will come to you tonight. I gladly accept the risks."

❧ 8 ❧

Adrian was a damned scoundrel, he knew that, but he could not regret what he had done. He had only intended to give Lady Venetia a means of escape, but after that brief kiss in the library, his body had overtaken his rational thoughts.

Once he had her close to him in the dark, he could pretend he was someone worthy of her, someone who could seduce her and bring her to pleasure like any good lover would. She had come apart so beautifully, and to learn that it was her first time to feel that release? He was surely damned for enjoying that as much as he did.

After he left her, he returned to the library to retrieve their dinner tray. There was no sign of Monty or his lover. Adrian brought the dishes to the kitchen, and Mrs. Webster handed him a cup of tea and a few biscuits as he sat down at the servants' table. Phillip was there, sewing a button onto a waistcoat for Lord William.

"How goes the lady watching?"

"Well enough. She is easy to please."

"Is she?" Phillip asked in a polite tone, but his eyes suggested something more mischievous in the question, given that Adrian's own words had foolishly opened the door for such a line of inquiry. He hadn't meant that she was easy to pleasure, but simply that she was easy to be around, easy to get along with.

"Yes," Adrian answered curtly, letting the other man know to be careful what he said. The rooms had ears, especially downstairs.

"Well, Mr. Reeves handled everything tonight at dinner with Benjamin and Edward." Edward was one of the younger footmen, only recently hired. He was only seventeen, but he was a hard worker.

"Glad to hear the boy did well."

"He did. Mr. Reeves puffed up with pride."

Adrian laughed at this. The butler was always proud when Hartland's servants made a good show performing their duties.

The two of them were quiet for a long moment before Phillip spoke again.

"Adrian, you will be careful, won't you?"

"I will."

"Good," Phillip said with a sigh. "Because Hartland wouldn't be the same without you."

Adrian hadn't considered that. "It's nice to know I would be missed."

"You would, so don't let your heart run away with you," Phillip warned. "It wouldn't be fair to her, or you."

"Right, well, I'm off to bed." Adrian left his friend alone and headed to his small shared bedroom. The room was dark when he entered. Benjamin stirred from under his sheets.

"That you, Adrian?"

He smiled at the younger man. "Yes. Go back to sleep."

Benjamin's bed creaked as he rolled over. Adrian removed his shoes and waistcoat and changed into his brown trousers and white lawn shirt. He lay on top of the covers and listened to Benjamin's quiet snores. He waited for what felt like ages before he slipped back out of bed and tiptoed out of the room. The servants' hall was dark, but he knew the steps and doorways by heart. It was not hard to navigate his way quietly upstairs.

The lamps in the gilded corridors burned low and created an eerie atmosphere, as though the portraits of Hartland's ancestors watched and judged him as he passed through the long picture gallery.

He comforted himself by thinking of the beautiful, openhearted lady who awaited him, and Lord Byron's words once more came to his mind:

It is the hour when from the boughs
The nightingale's high note is heard—
It is the hour—when lovers' vows
Seem sweet in every whisper'd word—
And gentle winds and waters near
Make music to the lonely ear.
Each flower the dews have lightly wet,
And in the sky the stars are met:
And on the wave is deeper blue,
And on the leaf a browner hue—
And in the Heaven, that clear obscure
So softly dark—and darkly pure,
That follows the decline of day
As twilight melts beneath the moon away.

Lady Venetia seemed to belong to a hundred poems by Byron, his words wrapping around her in an exquisite package, and tonight Adrian would bask in her womanly glow, consequences be damned. He didn't knock when he reached her bedchamber; he simply eased the door open and slipped inside. A lamp burned low on the bedside table nearest the door, and he saw Venetia lying in bed. Her face was turned toward him, her dark-brown eyes open.

"I'm sorry you had to wait so long," he apologized. "I know the routines of all the servants, and I had to be sure that I would not be seen." He came and sat down on the edge of the bed, feeling an undeniable excitement now that he was so close to taking this beautiful woman to bed.

She eased up so that she was sitting, and her hands fidgeted with the edge of the blue counterpane.

"You can change your mind at any time, my lady," Adrian said as he touched her hands with one of his, gently playing with her fingers.

"I haven't, but I am a ball of nerves. I have no idea what I'm doing. And . . . I want to make sure that this is what you want as well."

Adrian brushed his thumb over her inner wrist as he met her gaze. "From the moment you stepped out of your coach when you first arrived here, I have wanted nothing else but to be with you."

"Truly?" Her lashes lowered as she gazed down at their joined hands.

"Truly. And if you wish for me to simply hold you tonight, I will happily do that."

"That sounds lovely, and I should like that . . . after . . ." She reached up to the laces of her nightgown and tugged them free. The fabric of the nightgown loosened so that it draped off her shoulders. The pale, creamy skin she exposed set his pulse racing.

"I am not sure of what to do. Perhaps you could

take the lead?" She asked him this so sweetly that it almost killed him.

"I would be happy to. But you must promise to tell me to stop if you change your mind. Do you understand?"

Venetia nodded.

Adrian stood and pulled back the covers, exposing her to him. Her nightgown reached her shins, but it was thin enough that he could see her curves generously hinted at beneath the cloth. Adrian removed his boots, stockings, and shirt, laying them carefully on one of the chairs before he returned to the bed. Venetia had moved, sitting so that her lovely legs and dainty feet were draped over the edge. He stopped just in front of her and captured her hands, lifting them to his chest.

"First, you touch me," he said. He knew it would make it harder to focus, but he wanted her to feel like she had some control in this. Adrian believed that lovemaking was an act shared between two people, not one simply taking pleasure of another. And if this ended up being his only night with Venetia, he wanted it to be special.

VENETIA WAS HESITANT TO TOUCH ADRIAN'S BARE chest. He was so excruciatingly beautiful, like the

Adonis she'd first named him. Her palms slid up his chest, his warm skin enticing. She leaned in and rubbed her cheek against his chest. A light smattering of dark hair trailed from his upper chest and down below his navel, vanishing beneath the line of his trousers. She explored him, her body flushing with heat as she responded to him.

Adrian's fingers rubbed lightly over her skin as he stood there, letting her explore him. Then after a moment, he raised her chin and bent his head to capture her mouth. The kiss was languid, decadent. It was like biting into ripe strawberries and savoring their sugary sweetness. He gently bit her lower lip and flicked his tongue against hers in a playful rhythm that reminded her of what he had done with his fingers in the hidden passageway.

She was barely aware of him pulling at the edges of her loosened nightgown, slipping it down over her shoulders until it pooled around her waist. She gasped as one of his hands cupped her bare breast. He squeezed and rolled her sensitive nipple between his thumb and forefinger, causing a zing of harsh pleasure to shoot from the tip of her breast to her womb. She clutched at the strands of his dark hair, tangling her fingers in it as he continued to kiss her. A wetness pooled between her thighs, and she rubbed against him, trying to ease the growing need within her.

He broke the kiss, panting. Then he pushed her flat on the bed—not roughly, but with a possessive command that thrilled her. He gripped her night-gown, and she lifted her hips to allow him to remove it. Then he spread her thighs and leaned over her on the bed.

The cool night air drifted across her skin, cooling her just as his touch set her on fire all over again. Adrian kissed down her throat to her breasts, sucking at both nipples until she was hungry to feel his mouth in other wicked places. His hands were slightly rough to the touch, hands that had lived a life of work, hands that filled her with excitement and arousal. The thought of his strength and how he might over-power her with seduction was a fantasy she'd never indulged in until now.

She was suddenly shy, yet it was almost impossible to focus on the part of herself that wanted to conceal her nakedness. He ran his tongue inside her navel, then kissed down to her mound. She panted and trembled now as he parted her legs wider and covered her sensitive bud with his lips. She nearly screeched and bowed off the bed in shock at the violent yet pleasurable sensations his mouth caused between her legs. He chuckled against her in a wicked rumbling sound that was so utterly masculine and dominant that it made her head spin. He knew exactly what to do to drive a woman wild.

When he flicked his tongue against her folds, she had to cover her mouth with a balled fist to silence another scream. It was too much. The climax hit her hard, leaving her limp and breathless. She closed her eyes, feeling as though she were melting into the mattress beneath her. Then something nudged her entrance. She opened her eyes to see Adrian had removed his trousers, and his shaft, a glorious, long, intimidating bit of male anatomy, was pushing into her.

She was on the verge of tensing up when he thrust deep. Something tore inside her, and she whimpered as the pain radiated deep within her. He leaned over, whispering apologies and covering her face with kisses. The tenderness he showered her with in that frightening moment bonded her to him in a way she could never have imagined.

"Hush, my sweet love. Hush now, it's over." He nuzzled her ear before he kissed the sensitive spot behind it. Fresh desire awoke within her, and her inner walls clenched around his length. He groaned as though in pain.

"Are you all right?" she asked.

"Oh yes. It feels good when you do that."

"Do what?" She couldn't help but clench around him again.

"*That!* Bloody hell," he cursed and stole her lips for a long, deep, and raw kiss.

After a moment he began to move within her, thrusting slowly, easing her body into a natural, ancient rhythm. Venetia was still tender, but the sharp pain soon faded. Adrian pulled her closer to the edge of the bed, and she wrapped her legs around his waist as he continued to thrust into her. The feel of him filling her, that sense of connection, was beyond compare. Her next release built slowly, sweetly, and rippled out in a burst of pleasure that didn't quickly fade. Tears stung at her eyes as she gripped Adrian close to her.

His breath hitched, and he suddenly withdrew from her. Then he hissed and held her close, panting. Wetness coated her belly, and she gazed down at their bodies in confusion.

"I'm sorry," he whispered. "I wanted to stay inside you, but we can't risk getting you with child." He kissed her forehead tenderly, then moved away from her and retrieved a cloth from beside her water basin. He returned and wiped her belly and between her thighs. She blushed as he removed the evidence of blood and cleaned himself. After that, he tucked her back into bed. She nearly giggled at the thought of being completely naked like this. It was so very scandalous.

"You'll stay, won't you?" she asked as he laid the towel near his clothes.

"Yes, if you want me to."

She nodded and held out a hand to him. He slid into bed, and she sighed with contentment as she curled into him. She wasn't used to having such a warm, hard presence in her bed, but she definitely liked it. It was comforting. She felt safe in a way she'd never expected. Adrian stroked her hair, and she pressed a soft kiss to his chest.

"Thank you for showing me such a wonderful thing."

His chest rose and fell in a long inhalation. "And I thank you for giving me the gift of your maidenhead. I know I hurt you . . ."

"Only for a moment, and it was worth the pain. *You* are worth the pain."

She snuggled close to him, fatigue setting in amidst the afterglow of their lovemaking.

❦

ADRIAN STAYED AWAKE AWHILE LONGER, FEELING Venetia sleeping deeply in his arms. Her golden hair was pale and silky in the moonlight. He stroked it, tucking loose strands of hair behind her ear. He couldn't seem to stop touching her. He wanted to stay awake all night so he could watch her, hold her.

A smile curled Venetia's lips, and he wondered what pleasant dreams had drawn that smile out. She was so sweet and innocent, a *true* lady. He didn't believe, no matter how much Mr. Reeves drilled it into him, that lowborn people couldn't be ladies or gentlemen in their demeanor and bearing.

No, the true quality and ability of a person came from his or her soul. And there was no doubt that Venetia was a true lady. She was kind, openhearted, fair, and passionate. After tonight, he would do anything she asked of him, no matter what it cost him. He *belonged* to her. Though she would leave at the end of the week and he would likely never see her again, he knew his heart was hers forever. Come what may, Venetia owned his soul.

9

Adrian woke well before dawn, and he didn't immediately remember where he was. But the bed was so soft, the air fragrant with flowers, and the small body tucked into his side was most unexpected. Then the previous night came back to him in a wonderous and terrifying flash.

Venetia's face was pressed to his shoulder, and one of her arms was curled around his waist. He wanted to stay here *forever*. But he couldn't. He had to go. He had to get back downstairs before any of the other staff realized he hadn't slept in his own room last night.

Last night was a mistake; he would be terminated immediately if anyone found out. But he couldn't regret what he had done, not with her. Yet his livelihood was at stake, and he might end up paying for the rest of his life for one night with her.

He lifted Venetia's arm, slipped out of bed, and donned his clothes. The clock in the hall chimed four times. It was early enough that he could get safely downstairs without being seen. He rolled up the bloody cloth and carried it into the corridor with him. The house was still dark and quiet, and he moved briskly and almost soundlessly down the back stairs to the servants' hall, trying to look as though he was about his usual chores and not sneaking away from a lady's bedchamber. If no one saw him, everything would be all right.

The scullery maid had already lit the fire in the kitchen. He tossed the cloth onto it and used a poker to push it deep into the flames. He lingered a few moments, making sure the cloth was burned sufficiently. Disposing of that damning evidence took a weight off his mind.

When he opened the door to his bedchamber, he cursed. Benjamin was up, dressed, and staring at him with anxious eyes.

"Close the door," Benjamin said, his solemn tone not boding well.

Adrian did and leaned back against it.

"Where did you sleep?"

"Not here," Adrian said cautiously.

"Lady Venetia." Benjamin's reply was not a question. Adrian said nothing. "Damnation, Adrian. If Mr. Reeves finds out . . ."

"I know. He won't."

"You can't know that. The man has eyes in the back of his head. It takes only one night that you sleep in, one moment where a guest or a member of the staff sees you."

The confidence Adrian had been feeling was punctured effortlessly by Benjamin's words. But even though he tried to convince himself that he would stay away from Venetia's bed, he knew that if she wanted him, he'd come.

"I know, Benjamin, but I cannot deny her. She owns me."

"I know what part of you she owns," Benjamin said dryly.

"I am not under the thrall of my loins, Benjamin. She owns my heart, my spirit—you understand?"

Benjamin sighed heavily. "I understand that *you* believe that. But you're going to need help—*my* help —if you don't want to be caught."

Relief swept through him. Benjamin was a good man, a good friend.

"I would gladly accept any help."

Benjamin frowned. "Just remember that I'm sharing in the risk and getting none of the reward. You'd better change, or you will be late." He patted Adrian's shoulder as he passed by and left the room.

Adrian hurried into his livery and caught up with Benjamin to begin his daily duties. He would leave it up to Venetia to summon him again.

By midmorning, a hunting party had been announced as the day's primary activity, and Adrian had no chance to see Venetia. Every footman was required for such an event. He ran about the front lawn of the house, dodging prancing horses and handing goblets of wine to the men who sat on horseback.

Lord Devon, Mr. Sherman, and the other gentlemen all looked eager for the hunt. The hounds darted about the pebbled road, barking in excitement. A trio of ladies wearing fine riding habits joined the men and mounted their own horses before the hunt began.

The horses took off across the lawn toward the woods. The foxhounds led the way, baying in excitement. Adrian gave a sigh of relief as he and Benjamin carried their empty trays of glasses back inside. Mr. Reeves met them at the servants' entrance, ready with their next tasks.

"Lady Devon is having tea with the rest of the ladies in the picture gallery. Freshen up so that you don't smell of the stables, and then go and wait upon them."

"Yes, Mr. Reeves," they answered in unison. He and Benjamin changed their coats, brushed the dust off their breeches, and headed up to the long picture gallery.

The gilded room was filled almost floor to ceiling with pictures of the noble house of Devon's ancestors. He halted at the sight of Venetia standing among the beautifully dressed ladies, who were all gossiping. She stilled when she noticed him, her eyes lingering upon him before she turned back to the lady who was speaking to her.

"I'll take the east end, you the west," Benjamin whispered as he walked to the far edge of the gallery and took up his post.

Adrian did the same. His mind began to wander, but each stray thought seemed to bring him back to Venetia. She and her grandmother were deep in conversation with Lady Devon and Lady Mowbray.

He recognized who his half sister was the moment he saw her, spying hints of himself in her amber eyes and the way her mouth curved in a smile. And the dark hair piled atop her head in fashionable curls was the same rich dark color as his own. He tried desperately not to think about how his own flesh and blood stood not ten feet away. The woman knew nothing of him. She'd been born into a life of luxury and opportunity, while he was trapped, forever serving those like her.

He was as close to a statue as he could be, but his white-gloved hands curled into fists. This time stray thoughts of Venetia were welcome because they kept his rage at his father and grief for his mother at bay.

After a time, he became aware of a pair of eyes upon him. They were not Venetia's eyes, nor Lady Mowbray's. It was Mr. Sherman's sister, Mrs. Hamill. Her pale-blue eyes were fixed on him, and a hint of a smile was on her lips.

"Lady Devon. Would you mind terribly if I had your footman help me with something? My maid is likely having tea at this time, and I do not wish to disturb her," Mrs. Hamill said sweetly.

"Of course. Benjamin would—"

Mrs. Hamill nodded at Adrian. "Oh, but this one is much closer." Her words created a chill that raced along his skin. He knew just what sort of task she would need help with, and he had no desire to leave this spot.

"Adrian, would you please see to Mrs. Hamill?"

"Yes, your ladyship." Anxiety knotted inside him as he followed Mrs. Hamill out the door. He had seen that all too familiar look in her eyes from a dozen women before.

"This way," the woman called briskly. He followed her in the direction of the rooms on the second floor where most of the guests were staying. She opened her bedchamber door, glanced about to check that they were alone, and motioned for him to join her. He did so reluctantly. Mrs. Hamill closed the door behind him and turned the key in the lock.

"We must be quick, and do not muss my hair." She sat on the edge of the bed and started to lift her skirts.

"Madam, please—" Adrian nearly reached out to pull her skirts back down, but he had tried that once before with another woman, and it had made it nearly impossible to pry the lusty creature off him. It was wiser to keep his distance.

"Don't be silly. Come over here now," she commanded.

Adrian held back a retort that he was not some stud put in a paddock to breed. To her, he was.

"I apologize, but I cannot. Lady Devon does not allow guests and staff to—"

"She would rather have her guests needs satisfied. Isn't that correct?" Mrs. Hamill began to unfasten the buttons on the front of her gown. This was going to end badly, but he had to extricate himself.

"I'm happy to attend to any needs *other* than the ones your husband alone should see to."

The woman hissed like an angry cat. She grabbed a silver-handled hairbrush off a table and hurled it at him. He ducked as it collided against the wall, and he nearly broke the key as he violently twisted it in the lock to get free. He stumbled into the corridor and slammed the door shut behind him, then took off running. He had to put as much distance between him and Mrs. Hamill as possible. Adrian skidded to a stop at the top of the servants' stairs and leaned back against the wall, closing his eyes as he regained his breath.

"Adrian?" Mr. Reeves's tone held a note of suspicion.

Christ, he thought. *Never one bloody moment alone in this life.*

He opened his eyes and faced the butler. "Sir?"

"Shouldn't you be in the picture gallery with Benjamin?"

"I was called away to assist Mrs. Hamill with an errand." Adrian wanted to tell Mr. Reeves about Mrs. Hamill, but he feared that it would only make matters worse because Mr. Reeves would actually believe him, and having to meet with Lady Devon to tell her about a guest's attempt at seduction would be an uncomfortable discussion. They'd had to deal with this before. It wasn't something Adrian liked, and he and Mr. Reeves usually kept the matter between the two of them when they felt they could.

"I believe Benjamin has it handled for now. Is there anything I can do here, Mr. Reeves?" He nodded down the stairs toward the kitchens.

"You may help prepare the dining room for the ladies' luncheon," Mr. Reeves said.

With an air of relief, Adrian retreated to the

kitchens, where the aroma of roasted duck in orange marmalade welcomed him. He tried to push away thoughts of Mrs. Hamill and how she would no doubt seek out some kind of revenge. The question was, how and when would she strike?

VENETIA WATCHED THE DOOR OF THE LONG picture gallery, waiting for Mrs. Hamill and Adrian to return. Mrs. Hamill returned almost at once, but Adrian did not. Venetia tried to read the woman's expression. Mrs. Hamill was a pretty woman, auburn-haired with pale-blue eyes, but she wasn't the nicest of women. She was prone to gossip, at least according to Venetia's grandmother. Just then, Mrs. Hamill's lips were pinched into a tight pout, and her eyes grew hard as they swept the room. Venetia focused on the paintings, staying close to her grandmother and Lady Devon.

"What the devil is this one wearing?" Gwen pointed her cane at a portrait of a man from the 1620s. He wore breeches that stopped just above his knees and an ornate red velvet doublet. The breeches puffed out around his rather slender legs in a decidedly comical fashion.

"That is Sir Poncenby's ancestor. I can't recall his

name. I have no idea why we even have this portrait, to be honest."

"I mean, what is he on about with those ridiculous pants?" her grandmother asked. "Does he have pillows puffed inside there to protect his bony posterior when he sits down?"

Venetia stifled a giggle.

"I suppose the fashion was to appear like he was a Christmas turkey with two meaty thighs and bony little shins," Gwen mused.

Lady Devon bit her lip to hide a smile. "The Poncenbys have always been most interested in the latest fashion trends, even ill-advised ones."

"My dear," Gwen said to Lady Devon, "I would suggest packing that painting up at once and sending it back to Sir Poncenby. I feel that no matter where I stand"—Gwen moved back and forth, still looking at the painting—"those puffy breeches quite follow me about."

Lady Devon shared a twinkling gaze with Venetia. "I'll speak to my husband about the matter when he returns from the hunt."

Mrs. Hamill moved away from the main group of ladies to speak to Mrs. Leslie, her friend. The two tucked themselves into a corner and spoke in hushed tones. Venetia, being nearest to them, could make out parts of their conversation.

"Well?" Mrs. Leslie asked.

"He wouldn't. I insisted, but—he left me." Mrs. Hamill scowled at this.

"He refused you?"

"Yes."

The two ladies lowered their voices more, but Venetia was positive she knew what had happened. Mrs. Hamill had propositioned Adrian, and he had refused her. A dozen emotions fluttered inside Venetia—worry, anger, and frustration being the strongest. The thought of that woman—*any* other woman—kissing Adrian made her stomach upset.

She had no right to feel so possessive of him, but she did, and she despised herself for it. Was she any different from Mrs. Hamill? No, she wasn't. She was a selfish creature who had made Adrian come to her bed at great risk to his employment. She'd been so blinded by her newfound passions that she hadn't thought clearly about how he would feel about it, but that was no excuse. She had taken advantage of him through her position as a lady, and upon reflection it was wrong—terribly wrong.

Lady Devon announced lunch, and the women all left the picture gallery. Her grandmother fell in step beside her.

"What's the matter, my dear? You've gone quite pale. Is your ankle paining you?"

"It is," she admitted, but in truth the swelling had gone down quite a bit. It wasn't sharply painful like it had been. She was more troubled by a dull ache than anything else.

"Well, it will be good for you to sit and rest then," Gwen said as they entered the dining hall.

Venetia nearly stumbled when she saw Adrian setting up trays of food on the sideboard table. Shame curled around her heart and gripped it so tightly that she struggled to breathe. He looked so perfect in his gold-and-black livery, his dark hair falling across his eyes as he settled the tray into place. When he finished, he moved discreetly out of the way and settled into his post in the corner. He didn't look her way, yet she had the sense that he was aware of her, and that only made her guilt worse.

"Gran, I'm afraid I'm not feeling well. I think I shall lie down."

"You would feel better if you ate," Gwen said. "Ladies shouldn't be afraid to eat. There would be a lot less of those silly fainting spells if they did."

"I believe tight corsets play a part in that as well, Gran."

"Don't get me started on those. Ridiculous contraptions, wildly overused. You should have yours loosened immediately if you feel it might be to blame."

Venetia kissed her grandmother's cheek and made her excuses to Lady Devon before slipping out of the room. By the time she had reached the stairs, silly, childish tears coated her cheeks. She had been such a fool and an inconsiderate woman. She wouldn't summon Adrian again, no matter how much the thought broke her heart.

GWEN LIGHTLY TAPPED HER CANE AS SHE WAITED IN the small line to collect her lunch, but her mind was far from food. Something was wrong with Venetia, and it was not her ankle. She'd been fine until . . . Well, until Mrs. Hamill had left the room with the dashing footman who'd been tending to Venetia. Was it simple jealousy? Her granddaughter was not usually prone to such things. But it was easy to see how one could be jealous over a fine young man like Adrian.

She prepared her plate and moved to the table. Adrian stepped up to pull her seat out for her, and she crooked a finger at him so that he leaned down to her level.

"Could you see to Lady Venetia? She is ill, and I am most worried."

A spark of concern lit Adrian's eyes. He nodded and left immediately. When Gwen turned back to the table, she saw Mrs. Hamill watching her with a calculating gleam in her stare. Gwen stared back sternly. Mrs. Hamill flinched, and Gwen raised her chin in victory. There was no man or woman who hadn't backed down when Gwen set that stare on them.

"Now, Lady Devon, when can we expect the rest of our party back from all that hunting nonsense?"

ADRIAN KNOCKED ON VENETIA'S DOOR. THERE WAS a moment of silence before she answered.

"Who is it?"

"Adrian, your ladyship. Lady Latham sent me to see if you are all right."

The long silence that followed filled him with dread. He hadn't liked how pale Venetia had been in the dining room, and he'd never been more relieved to receive Lady Latham's orders to go and check on her.

"Please go away. I am quite fine." Her voice was stilted, unnatural, which made his concern only deepen. Taking the risk of upsetting her, he opened the door.

Venetia sat in a chair by the unlit fireplace, wiping tears from her eyes. When he closed the door, she glanced up at him and then burst into tears again. Adrian rushed to her side and knelt by the chair, taking her hands in his.

"What's the matter?"

She shook her head and refused to meet his eyes.

"Please, my love, tell me," he begged. "You are destroying me with your tears." He wiped at her eyes with his fingertips.

"I can't," she whispered.

"Are you in pain? Should I send for the doctor?"

She shook her head frantically. "No, no, it isn't that."

Adrian was overstepping his bounds, but he couldn't bear to see her suffer. He lifted her up from the chair and took her place, then pulled her onto his lap so he could hold her in his arms. She was trembling.

"Venetia, tell me what's wrong."

She placed a hand on his chest. Her fingers splayed over the gold-and-black striped waistcoat of his uniform. Her breath hitched. "You must despise me—that's all I can think."

"What? Why would I?"

Tears clung to her thick dark-gold lashes. "I am no better than Mrs. Hamill," she sniffled. "I ordered you to my bed and put your employment at risk."

Comprehension dawned on him. He couldn't help but smile, and when she noticed, her brow wrinkled in confusion.

"My lady." His voice softened as warm emotions burrowed deep inside him. "You and Mrs. Hamill are not the same, certainly not to me. She tried to order me to bed her, but I refused, and I fear she's quite furious with me. But that has nothing to do with you. What lies between us . . ." He paused, tongue-tied by this beautiful, compassionate woman. "What we have is special. I have never done this with any other houseguest. And I have never felt this way about any woman. I am willing—*more* than willing—to do anything with you, anything *for* you. Do you understand?"

Venetia was slow to nod, but her brown eyes, such a lovely rich color, were wide and a little stunned. That was good. It meant she finally understood the depth of his devotion.

"Are we mad, Adrian? To feel so deeply after only a few days?"

"If we are, then I shall seek no treatment for such madness." He brushed his thumb along the delicate line of her jaw and down to her lips. Touching her was such a pleasure, he still couldn't believe it. He wished he never had to stop.

"Now dry your eyes, love. You must return to the luncheon so that your grandmother does not worry anymore."

"And you? What will you do?"

"I will resume my duties and avoid Mrs. Hamill and her hairbrushes."

"Hairbrushes?" Venetia asked as she played with the folds of his neckcloth.

"She threw a hairbrush at my head when I refused her."

"Oh heavens." Venetia did not wish to laugh at Adrian's plight, but she did, and soon her eyes were bright with joy again.

"I shall come to you tonight if you wish, and you can regale me with all the gossip I don't hear while on duty."

"And I promise not to throw any hairbrushes at you." Venetia leaned in and kissed him.

He claimed her lips in return, wanting so much to carry her to bed, but he couldn't be gone much longer. He was falling in love with this woman, and it was indeed like falling. He was out of control, and his heart was so full of her that he didn't care what happened when he hit the ground. She was worth everything.

The rest of the week was uneventful. He had no more unwanted encounters with Mrs. Hamill, and he spent so much time in bliss with Venetia. Adrian could scarcely believe how easy it was to be with her, to be himself and not carry any shame of his past with him because she knew the truth and didn't care. Although Mr. Sherman continued to pay court to Venetia during the day, Adrian was able to witness that she had no real interest in the man aside from his friendship. It was a small thing, but it gave Adrian hope, hope for what he was too afraid to voice aloud.

Whenever he had a spare moment, he sought her out, under the guise of bringing her tea or running an errand for her. It gave him a dozen small moments to touch her, to secretly kiss her, to whisper questions about her life and she of his. It hadn't been easy to tell her so much about himself—he wasn't used to sharing his life with anyone—but she never judged him or looked down upon him, as many people in her position often did.

Venetia had a brilliant mind for politics and economics, and her voracious love of reading was something that he shared. She was also playful, teasing him so much during a game of cards that he lost his focus and they both dissolved into laughter. In these moments, he forgot that he was a man from belowstairs rather than her equal, a gentleman.

And he had seen in the last few days how she had blossomed under his attentions. Her shyness had faded away, and he could see the humorous and clever woman her grandmother so clearly adored.

Adrian joined Venetia in bed each night, making love to her and sharing more stories of his life and she of hers until he felt he knew her better than anyone at Hartland. He also learned more of the intimidating Lady Latham and how she fiercely loved Venetia and had a soft heart beneath that fire-breathing exterior.

"Your grandmother really wants someone to thrash your cousin?"

They lay together in the predawn darkness, chuckling over what Venetia had just told him.

"Oh yes. Patrick is odious, and Gran is quite

serious about someone putting him in his place." Venetia's tone turned more solemn. "Before we left for this party, he was positively frightening."

A dark cloud of fury began to gather inside Adrian. "Did he hurt you?"

"Not really. He grabbed my arms and gave me a good shaking. I don't know what he might have done to me if Gran hadn't stepped in and used her cane like a fencing foil." A faint smile hovered about Venetia's lips. "After that, we knew we had to leave. I have no doubt that he has some wretched scheme to marry me off when we return."

Adrian was quiet a long moment. He understood Venetia's predicament. She had to marry quickly and couldn't afford to choose her husband poorly. But the thought of a man marrying her, even a decent one like Peregrine Sherman, made Adrian's stomach turn. For a moment he imagined himself carrying Venetia across the threshold of a small country cottage bedecked with flowers and sprawling ivy, a wedding bouquet grasped in her hands. She would be safe with him, safe in his world, far from her cousin. But that was a foolish dream that he couldn't indulge in.

"I need to get up," he sighed.

Venetia feathered kisses on his bare chest. "Perhaps you could stay another few minutes?" Venetia giggled as he rolled her beneath him. He parted her thighs and sank into her welcoming flesh, sharing a soft moan with her as he kissed her passionately. It was so easy to love her, both with his heart and his body. He rode her slowly, enjoying the soft gasps and quickened breaths that escaped her as he claimed her. When he started to feel the rush of a climax, he tried to pull out of her.

"No, not yet." She wrapped her legs tighter around his waist.

"But—"

"Adrian." She spoke his name with an intensity that confused him. "*Please . . .*" She stroked the back of his neck, and he was lost to her plea. He continued to move within her, and she cried out so sweetly with her pleasure that the sound of it alone broke him of his restraint, and he joined her in that headlong rush of physical joy.

He collapsed upon her, breathing harshly, just barely stopping himself from crushing her as he buried his face in her neck.

The shock of what had just happened sank in. He'd released himself inside her. She could be with child soon—his child. The thought brought both agony and joy to him all at once.

"What have we done?" he whispered.

She stroked his hair, seemingly unconcerned. "Whatever comes, I have no regrets. Not with you." She met his gaze, and he saw that she had made a decision about something, though he didn't know what. He started to speak, but she covered his lips with hers, blanking all thoughts from his mind as he lost himself in her kiss.

"You had better go. I will see you tonight."

She kissed him once more, and he tasted a promise there, but the meaning behind it eluded him.

He left the bed, dressed, and pressed one more quick kiss to her lips before he left the room. His keen eyes searched all the hallways, but he found no one watching. Only then did he feel safe to make the quick dash belowstairs. Once in the servants' hall, he began his day, and he had only just finished his breakfast when Mr. Reeves came into the kitchens, grumbling.

"Bloody rain. It will keep them all indoors and in foul moods," the butler muttered.

"It will," Adrian agreed. "Best to have the drink carts filled and ready."

"Yes, good idea, Adrian. Please see to it." The butler went into his office.

Adrian saw to his duties about the house. As Mr. Reeves had expected, the gentlemen spent the day inside playing cards and drinking. The ladies joined them for some of the card games when they were not gossiping over tea.

He did his best not to look in Venetia's direction, but he could feel her gaze drifting toward him a little too often. It was impossible to ignore her—she was so beautiful it hurt. And her beauty had very little to do with her fair hair or brilliant brown eyes. It was the way she smiled, the way she laughed, the way she spoke of the things she loved and was interested in. She was beautiful, and he would have given her the world if he'd been able to. He carefully avoided looking back. He would have to remind her to be careful. The languid heat he'd seen in her gaze when she looked at him might be noticed amongst these watchful women.

Midafternoon, Mr. Reeves appeared in the kitchen doorway while Adrian searched for a tea tray. Adrian stilled as he noticed the butler watching him. A frown marred the man's solemn countenance.

"Is something wrong, Mr. Reeves?"

"Montague. My office. *Now*."

Adrian shared a glance with the cook. Mrs. Webster's lips pursed into a worried frown as she looked at him. Being called by his surname did not bode well. Adrian saw that Benjamin had charge of the tea tray before he went to Mr. Reeves's office and knocked.

"Come." Mr. Reeves was standing in the corner of his office, and to Adrian's surprise, Lord Devon was there as well. Both men were frowning at Adrian. Dread knocked the wind from Adrian's lungs.

No, this can't be happening.

"Adrian, I have been informed that you've been

fraternizing with one of the guests. You know my policy on that." Lord Devon's eyes were heavy with sorrow and disappointment. Somehow, disappointing Lord Devon made this truly dreadful moment a thousand times worse.

"Your Grace, I'm sorry." He didn't try to make excuses. It would only make him look a fool.

"I'm afraid we must end your employment, effective immediately. I hate to send you away, Adrian. You've been a damned good footman, impeccable service, and Reeves said you've done so much to mentor the younger lads here. He fought for you to stay, but I fear we can't ignore the complaint."

That surprised Adrian. Mr. Reeves had fought for him? "I understand, Your Grace."

Mr. Reeves looked deeply troubled. "Well, in light of your years of service, I will provide a recommendation." He held out a sealed letter to Adrian, who took it with a numbness that left him beyond cold.

"Reeves will see you on your way. I am sorry, Adrian. Lady Devon and I will miss you."

Shame burned a hole through Adrian's chest. He bowed his head as Lord Devon left the butler's office. Mr. Reeves cleared his throat, and Adrian lifted his head.

"Sir, may I inquire as to who made the complaint?"

"It was Mrs. Hamill. She claims to have spotted you leaving Lady Venetia's bedroom this morning."

Of course. Mrs. Hamill had found a way to avenge her pride at last. He should have expected this. But he and Venetia had been so careful.

"Sir, you should know that Mrs. Hamill attempted to seduce me, and I believe she did this out of a desire to avenge her wounded pride."

"That may be the case, but the die is cast, and you did sleep with Lady Venetia."

"I know," he sighed. "But watch out for the other footmen. I don't want Mrs. Hamill to destroy any more lives."

"Agreed," Mr. Reeves said. "I will watch out for them. There is a coach leaving for London in half an hour. The driver has agreed to take you on the top seat if you can be ready."

"I can." Adrian swallowed hard. "Thank you for defending me, sir."

"I don't agree with his lordship on this. Lady Devon placed you in a difficult position. I was young once, and I remember how complicated situations like this can be." Mr. Reeves's sincerity only made this worse.

"You . . . ?"

Mr. Reeves nodded. "I also fell in love once with a lady above stairs."

Mr. Reeves had been in love with someone? Until

that moment, Adrian couldn't have pictured the grumpy butler as a dashing buck with romance on his mind and heart. Mr. Reeves understood, then, the knifing pain that Adrian was feeling in his chest and the way it was constricting his breathing.

"Sir . . . How did you recover?"

"A man doesn't recover, not from that. I moved on with all but my heart. That's all I will say on the matter. You had better go and pack your things."

Adrian entered his basement room, shoving his belongings into his old leather valise. He had few possessions, only a few books, a miniature of his mother, and a handful of his own clothes. For a lifetime of twenty-nine years, he had so little. It bothered him more now than ever to have so little evidence of a life lived.

But he also had one handkerchief, one that Venetia had embroidered for him a few days ago. He rubbed his thumb over the intricate ivy leaves surrounding his initials: *A. M.* It was such a small gift from her, yet to him it was the only thing that mattered, aside from his mother's small gilt-framed likeness.

"So it's true—you're leaving," Benjamin said from the doorway. The young man's face was stricken. Adrian hadn't realized how much Benjamin looked up to him. Leaving Hartland, leaving his friends—it was going to be harder than he ever thought.

"Yes," Adrian answered slowly, doing his best to keep emotion out of his voice. "Mrs. Hamill was furious that I did not accept her gracious offer to bed her, and now she has her revenge." Adrian had no desire to hold his tongue now. It wasn't as though things could get worse. He'd already been terminated.

"It's a bloody unfair business." Benjamin looked furious.

"It is. But life is unfair, at least to our kind." Adrian tucked the handkerchief safely in his bag and headed toward the door.

Benjamin held out his hand. "Write to me. Let me know where you've settled."

"Yes, of course," Adrian promised.

He left his room and found that many of the servants were there to see him off, including Mr. Reeves.

Mrs. Webster embraced him. "Good luck, lad."

Phillip shook Adrian's hand, echoing his mother's sentiments.

The coach was waiting out front. Adrian climbed onto the top seat, pulling his cloak tightly about him as it began to rain. He hadn't had a chance to say goodbye to Venetia, but that was for the best. They had both been living in a dream this last week. Better to simply vanish and leave behind only golden-hued memories. He would carry her in his heart forever, and that would have to be enough. Memories of her sunny hair, the sound of her laugh, the way she lost herself when she was reading aloud to him, the way she looked into his eyes with such adoration that for one brief week he had felt truly, deeply, earnestly *loved*.

VENETIA WATCHED THE RAINDROPS TRAIL DOWN the windowpane of the drawing room and sighed. Mr. Sherman and a few others were playing a game of faro, and some ladies, including her grandmother, were conversing in another corner of the room. The outdoor picnic planned for today had been canceled due to the poor weather. While Venetia enjoyed plenty of indoor activities, she had been looking forward to being outside for a bit.

It was silly, but she'd been hoping to steal away with Adrian in the garden hedges, perhaps steal a few kisses, and watch the sun light up his face. Whenever he was alone with her, he opened up in the most marvelous way that left her breathless. She longed to see that part of him again, to see him playful and happy—and *hers*.

A nagging feeling pulled her from her daydreams. She glanced about the room and noticed that Mrs. Hamill was watching her with a smug look on her face. Lord Devon came into the room, and Lady

Devon excused herself to speak with him in hushed tones. The duchess's gaze flicked to Venetia and then back to her husband. Mrs. Hamill got up from her seat and came to sit beside Venetia. The woman's catlike smile made the hairs on Venetia's neck stand on end.

"Such a pity," the other woman said. Her tone conveyed an acidic victory that distressed Venetia.

"What is?" she asked.

"That handsome footman, the tall one with the dark hair? Lord Devon sent him packing."

At first the words didn't quite register in Venetia's mind. "Sent him packing?"

"Yes," Mrs. Hamill replied with a sharp smile. "He's been intimate with one of the guests." She leveled Venetia with a pointed stare. Nausea churned in Venetia's stomach. "I just had to inform His Grace when I saw the man's indiscretion. He left a short while ago."

Venetia's mind ran at a frantic pace. Adrian had been let go? He was already gone? Fury and fear dueled within her, leaving her unsure of what to do, until at last anger triumphed. Venetia reached for her cold, abandoned cup of tea, stood, and without a word poured the contents on Mrs. Hamill's head. The woman shrieked and flapped her arms like a soaked chicken.

"Why, you—"

"Careful, Mrs. Hamill," Venetia warned. "Or I will tell everyone in this room *why* you went running to Lord Devon about Mr. Montague." She *tsked*. "Throwing hairbrushes like a spoiled child." Mrs. Hamill hissed like an angry cat before she flounced from the room.

Her grandmother had risen from her chair at the sign of the argument. "Venetia, dear, one is supposed to drink tea, not pour it over the heads of simpering fools. Though I do understand the impulse."

"I'm sorry, Gran. It slipped."

Gwen gave a thin smile. "Did it now?"

Mr. Sherman glanced between Venetia and where his sister had gone with open concern.

Venetia crossed the room, aware of the entire assembly now watching her. "Lord Devon, may I speak to you?"

The duke nodded gravely and stepped into the corridor with her.

"Is it true that you've dismissed Mr. Montague?"

The duke's face turned a ruddy red. "Er . . . Yes, unfortunately."

"You should know that Mrs. Hamill attempted to coerce him into her bed, and she came to you to have him dismissed after he turned her down."

This took the duke by surprise. "I was not aware of that. Then you deny that you had an indiscretion with the man?"

"I do not deny it." Venetia wouldn't deny it. It would be an insult to Adrian to pretend, when he'd already suffered the consequences of their secret love affair.

"Then I fear my actions must stand, and I suspect your grandmother will have much to say to you about this matter."

In that moment, Venetia had a brilliant flash of clarity. She could see a future she had not been brave enough to fully envision before. A future where she spoke her vows in a church to the only man she knew was worth marrying. She saw amber-eyed babes. She saw light and laughter in her life. She saw Adrian.

"Has he already gone?" she asked Lord Devon.

"He is on a coach heading for London. Mr. Grimsby had to leave the party a day early."

"I see . . ." Venetia was debating what to do, when the drawing room door opened and Mr. Sherman joined them.

"Lady Venetia, I sense that my sister has caused you some distress. Is there anything I might do to make amends?" The gentleman seemed completely sincere, and that gave her a spark of inspiration.

"Actually, yes. My ankle is still not up to riding on my own, but I desperately need to catch up with a coach on the road. Could you help me?"

"Of course."

"Thank you." She looked to Lord Devon. "I am

bringing him back, and I would greatly appreciate it if you would treat him well until I'm able to pack and leave with him."

"Leave . . . with him?" Lord Devon echoed uncertainly. "I'm not sure I understand."

Venetia's heart was beating wildly now. "I've decided to marry him." She said this with a smile that made her feel like she was glowing from within. *Marry Adrian*—yes, that was what she was going to do.

For a moment the duke simply stared at her. "I . . . Yes, yes, you can come back, of course. I like the man, Lady Venetia. It upset me greatly to have to send him away, but your grandmother . . ."

Venetia didn't have time to listen. She started toward the front door, Mr. Sherman at her side.

"So you have made a choice?" he said quietly. "I had rather hoped . . . But no matter. The best man won, and I am happy to help you."

"You know, then?" she asked.

Mr. Sherman instructed a footman to go to the stables and have his horse brought round as quickly as possible. He smiled sadly. "It was hard not to see. It was obvious that you were in love—it just wasn't with me."

She put a hand on his arm. "I am sorry, Mr. Sherman."

"Don't be, Lady Venetia. I confess that there wasn't as much of a spark as I had hoped for."

"And there should be, shouldn't there?"

"In the best marriages, yes. I had hoped that you and I might find a spark, but it seems you are destined for that footman."

A groom walked up with a horse, and Mr. Sherman went down the steps toward it. "Allow me to mount you up first."

Mr. Sherman handed her up. The saddle was already slick with rain, but Venetia didn't care. She held the reins while Mr. Sherman got up behind her. He wrapped his arms around her to grasp the reins, and they took off down the road. Neither of them spoke, and the rain grew heavier. Venetia was soon chilled to the bone, and after nearly a quarter of an hour she was afraid that they might not catch up with the coach.

Mr. Sherman raised a hand. "There!"

The black shape that was visible through the rain was indeed a coach.

Mr. Sherman called out to the coachman as he moved his horse closer. "Hello there! Please stop!"

The driver jerked on the reins, and the coach rolled to a stop. A man on top, covered in a rain-slicked cloak, sat hunched forward, unmoving. The driver, lower down on the front of the vehicle, turned to look at them.

"What's the matter, sir?" the driver asked.

"We're looking for a Mr. . . ." Mr. Sherman looked at Venetia uncertainly.

"Mr. Adrian Montague," she supplied.

"Mr. Adrian Montague. Is he on your coach?"

At Sherman's question, the figure sitting atop turned around. It was Adrian. Her beautiful footman, his face white with shock.

"My lady?" he gasped.

"Oh, Adrian! Please do come down. We must speak."

"I cannot. I'm bound for London. Lord Devon terminated my employment."

"I know, but it doesn't matter. Please come down from there."

Adrian gave an apologetic look to the coach driver as he climbed down and removed his valise from the back of the conveyance. He looked between her and Mr. Sherman in concern.

Mr. Sherman raised his hands. "I am here on a mission for love, but I am not in the way, I assure you."

The driver called out, "Oi! You staying or coming with us?"

"He's staying!" Venetia called back and waved the man away. For a moment she feared that Adrian would reject her words, reject her, but she had to trust that he loved her as she loved him.

"I am?" Adrian asked with heart-wrenching uncertainty.

The rain lessened a little. Venetia shivered, and Adrian removed his cloak and put it around her shoulders. His scent enveloped her, and she couldn't help but beam at him in relief. She'd found him. He hadn't vanished.

The coach driver shrugged and pulled away, leaving Venetia, Mr. Sherman, and Adrian with only one horse between them.

"Heavens, how are we to get back?" she asked.

"You'll ride," both men insisted. Venetia considered arguing, but she saw the resolve on their faces. There would be no arguing with them.

"Very well." She was lifted up into the saddle. Mr. Sherman took the reins and led the horse. They had walked only a few minutes when another coach approached them, this one with Venetia's family crest emblazoned on it.

"Lady Latham sent me for you, my lady!" the coachman said. "She didn't want you to get wet." The driver chuckled as he looked at the already soaked trio.

Mr. Sherman turned to Venetia as she slid out of the saddle and into Adrian's arms. "You and Mr. Montague need some time alone to converse. I shall ride back to the house ahead of you."

Venetia caught his hand. "Mr. Sherman, you are a

fine gentleman. There is a woman out there for you, a lady deserving of your noble heart." She smiled at him, and then with a grin she added, "But it would be best to keep her far away from your sister when you find her."

Mr. Sherman laughed heartily. "Never has truer advice been offered. I wish you all the best, Lady Venetia."

"I wish that for you as well."

Mr. Sherman left, and Venetia turned to Adrian, who had opened the coach door for her. She quickly climbed inside, and he followed.

"Venetia, why did you come after me?"

ADRIAN GAZED AT THE WOMAN WHO HELD HIS heart in her hands as she climbed inside the coach. She'd come for him, but why? Had she learned of his firing and convinced Lord Devon to reinstate him? Yet Mr. Sherman had said this was a mission of love. He wasn't trying to be deliberately obtuse, but sanity had to tamp down on the rising swell of hope within him. She couldn't be here for him, and yet . . .

He climbed inside the coach after her. "Venetia, why did you come after me?"

"I know that what I'm about to do is completely

out of the normal way of things, but I believe you would not ask, so I must."

"Ask what?" He studied her face, the way she looked so nervous and excited all at once.

"I came so that I could propose to you. Adrian, will you honor me for the rest of the days of our lives by marrying me?"

Adrian wondered if he'd fallen from the top of the coach and hit his head. He must be dreaming.

"I . . ."

Venetia's face reddened. "Heavens, if you don't want to, I understand, but I had thought that . . . Oh, I am silly, aren't I?"

She looked humiliated, and Adrian's reactions finally caught up with him. He reached across the seat to her, clasping her gloved hands in his. "The answer is yes. *Yes* to anything you might ever ask me," he replied, fighting off waves of powerful emotions that threatened to sweep him away.

She brightened with fresh hope. "Yes?"

"Yes, my heart, yes." He had no other words to tell her what lay in his heart, but *yes* was enough for now. Someday he would find the right romantic phrases a man like Mr. Sherman would speak to her, but for now all he had was *yes*.

The coach soon stopped in front of Hartland Abbey. "Are you certain that I am the right man?

Have you thought about what it would cost you to . . . marry beneath you?" he asked.

She leaned in to kiss him, her hands cupping his face. "I have, and I'm more certain than anything else in my life that this is what I want. I only wish I had been brave enough to ask you earlier."

"What stopped you?"

"The children. It won't be easy, but I believe that, given time, the scandal will pass and our children will be able to enter society with little gossip."

"Because of my birth and occupation?" He had never been more ashamed of himself than he was at that moment.

"Yes, but as I told you, I do not care about that. I care about *you*, the type of man you are, and I am ready to fight the world for you, Adrian. A few gossiping women don't stand a chance against me, my love. I have too much of Gran in me."

He studied the earnest determination in her eyes. "Those poor gossiping women," he teased.

"Poor indeed. And I shall be rich in my love for you." She kissed him again, her mouth soft upon his lips in a way that made him lightheaded. "Now, be brave. We must next face my grandmother."

Adrian assisted Venetia out of the coach, and they walked up the front steps of the Abbey. For the first time in all the years he'd lived at Hartland, he would be entering through the front door of his home.

"I believe your grandmother is the only person I fear."

"And rightly so." Lady Latham harrumphed as she met them inside the door.

"Lady Latham." Adrian bowed his head respectfully.

"Come in and dry off, you two." She frowned at Venetia. "What's gotten into you? Rushing off into the rain without a cloak like that. Smart young ladies chasing after men *always* take a coach and a cloak. If I hadn't had a coach, I never would have chased your grandfather down. Dear heavens, the man was practically running to get away from me, but I caught him in the end."

"But, Gran—" Venetia began to argue, only to stop and wonder what her grandmother and grandfather's love story was.

"I agree with her, Venetia. You're acting like one of Mrs. Radcliffe's Gothic novel heroines. All you are missing is your candelabra."

"Smart man, agreeing with me," Lady Latham said. "You chose well, my dear." Her tone toward Venetia warmed. "Now go upstairs and change. I need to have a word with Mr. Montague."

Venetia gave him an apologetic nod before rushing upstairs.

"In here." Lady Latham pointed her cane toward the nearest room, a small salon. She took a seat on the settee, but Adrian remained standing respectfully in her presence.

"You know of Venetia's situation?"

"Yes. She has told me why she wishes to marry someone of her own choosing, and why it has to be soon."

"She comes with a great deal of money and an oaf of a cousin who will likely cause problems, at first, for whoever she marries."

Adrian nodded. "She did mention that as well."

"If you marry her, you will face scrutiny and judgment at every turn." Lady Latham's tone was deadly serious. "Are you prepared for that? Even your children will face challenges."

"Yes."

"That being said, I have a few ideas that might help." She looked toward the doorway behind him and waved her hand, bidding someone to enter. He turned, and his heart caught in his throat.

Lady Mowbray, his half sister, stood before him. Her eyes searched his face before she smiled hesitantly.

"Adrian, is it?" his sister asked.

"Yes. How . . . ?"

"I claim the credit of that discovery, my boy," Lady Latham said. "Lady Devon did not divulge your parentage, no matter how much I pestered her, and that was quite a bit. No, it was the way Venetia watched Lady Mowbray with so much interest. And when we stood in the portrait gallery this morning, I realized that you bear a strong resemblance to my friend here. We put the pieces together while Venetia was off fetching you." Lady Latham smiled as her deductions were proved correct.

"Is it true?" Lady Mowbray asked. "My governess was your mother?"

"Yes," he said quietly. His heart and head filled with a soft fluttering that was somewhere between joy and panic.

Lady Mowbray's smile became more confident. "My brother and I adored your mother. I am sorry to hear that she passed." The beautiful woman turned her amber eyes on him, eyes they shared. "My father made a mistake in sending her away. He should have married her, and you should have had a childhood with us." She held out a hand to him. "You are family, at least to me, and I believe my brother will feel the same. Will you accept me . . . brother?"

Lady Mowbray's words and the olive branch of her hand were almost too much to bear. In one day, he had lost his entire world and now a new world and a new future had been thrust on him, one that was brighter than he ever could have dreamed.

"I am honored, Lady Mowbray."

"Ellen, please. We are family." She grinned, and Adrian clasped her hand between both of his.

"So, you see, my boy, your sister and I will do all within our power to bring you into the world, but it will still be a challenge."

"I understand," he replied. "Venetia is worth everything."

The older woman gave a cunning smile. "Good. Now you see why I chose you."

"Chose me?" he echoed in complete confusion.

Lady Latham laughed. "Yes, you think this was all fate and destiny? Dear boy, I knew from the moment you helped me from the coach when we first arrived that you would suit my granddaughter perfectly. It was just a matter of finding a way to pair you with her."

Lady Mowbray giggled and locked her arm with Adrian's. "It's best not to ask how Lady Latham works her magic," she whispered. "Lord Mowbray and I would not have gotten married if not for her clever intervention. Now come, let us talk while we wait for Venetia. We have much to catch up on, brother, and I wish to introduce you to my darling husband, Edward."

A drian stood in the small Hartland church close to the property of the Abbey, his friend Benjamin at his side. He wore a pair of fine dark-blue trousers and a matching coat with a gold waistcoat.

It felt odd not to be wearing the livery of a foot-man, which he'd worn nearly every single day of service, except on rare holidays. Ahead of him, the church was filled with a small group of Hartland Abbey servants, as well as Lord and Lady Devon and their children. It was alarming to be so visible after so many years of practicing the art of invisibility.

He looked toward Peregrine Sherman, who'd ridden to London with him two days before to procure a special license from the Doctors' Commons so he could marry Venetia straightaway.

He owed the man much and hoped to repay the favor someday. Peregrine nodded at him in silent acknowledgment.

"Steady on, old boy," said Benjamin.

"What if she changes her mind?" Adrian asked. "What if she realizes that she's made a mistake?"

"She's definitely making a mistake in marrying you, but I doubt that will stop her from showing up." His friend chuckled.

"You are such a balm to my ego," Adrian retorted.

The church doors opened before Adrian could reply. First, his half sister entered. Ellen shot him a bright smile as she found her place in the front pew. Adrian's half brother, Lord Bainbridge, followed behind her, Venetia upon his arm, escorting her down the aisle.

Part of him still wondered if he was dreaming. Had his life changed so dramatically in just a few short days? Had he been thrown from that carriage three days before, and now he was lying senseless upon a muddy road, and all of this was his imagination? He was lost for words as his future wife came toward him. He was marrying a lady, the daughter of an earl, and she *loved* him.

Venetia was a vision in blue watered silk, trimmed in Belgian lace. A small diadem of diamonds, a family heirloom, rested upon her golden hair. She was halfway down the aisle when the door at the back of the church flew open and a man rushed in. No, *barged* in. Stormed the church like it was the Bastille.

"Stop! I will not allow this!" The man charged toward Venetia, and she went stark white. He grasped her arm, twisting it. Adrian dashed down the aisle and jerked her free of the man, putting Venetia safely behind him.

"Who are you, sir, and why have you put your hands on my wife?" Adrian snarled.

The man glared hatefully over Adrian's shoulder at Venetia.

"She's not your wife yet. I am her cousin, and I have a say in who she marries. And it certainly won't be to some bastard like you!"

Adrian curled his hands into fists, ignoring the anxious stares of the wedding guests all around them.

"You must be Lord Latham, the *oafish* cousin I've heard so much about."

Adrian heard Lady Latham snort somewhere behind him.

Venetia's hand pressed lightly against his back, giving him silent support as she spoke to her cousin.

"Patrick, you must leave. I reached the age of majority three years ago. I do not need anyone's permission to marry, least of all yours." Venetia's voice was calm, but Adrian could feel a slight trembling in her as she pressed against him from behind.

"Think carefully, cousin," Patrick warned. "I'm a

peer now. You will lose *all of your friends and connections, and I will make sure you aren't welcome anywhere.* Your children will be the product of a bast—"

Adrian hit Patrick square in the jaw. The man yelped and staggered back, clutching his face.

"You've just assaulted a peer of the realm! I could see you hanged!" Patrick snapped.

Peregrine stepped up beside Adrian. "I don't see how, Latham. After all, you hit your face on the edge of a pew when you tripped while attending your beloved cousin's wedding. Very unfortunate."

"What!" Patrick shouted. "No one would agree to lie—"

Peregrine glanced around. "Did anyone see this man struck by a fist?" Not a single wedding guest made a sound. "Did anyone see him trip?" They all stared contemptuously at Patrick, and a rumble of agreement rolled through the pews.

Peregrine smiled grimly. "I believe it's time you left." He bent, gripped Patrick's arm, and dragged him toward the exit at the rear of the church.

"Oh, Adrian," Venetia whispered. "I'm so sorry about this."

Adrian gently took his fiancée's hands and smiled at her, letting her know all was well. With a look to Lord Bainbridge, who nodded in approval, Adrian walked Venetia to the altar himself.

The clergyman cleared his throat. "Let us begin."

Adrian held Venetia's hands in his, speaking his vows and listening to hers. Once it was done, he stole a kiss that made Benjamin cheer. Then they turned to face the assembled guests in the church, seeing the servants of Hartland who had been his family these last ten years, as well as the Duke and Duchess of Devon, who beamed at him with pride. His gaze fell last on Venetia's grandmother, who wiped a tear from her wrinkled cheek.

"Well done, my boy," she said. "Very well done."

Adrian's throat tightened as he realized that in her way, Lady Latham was saying that she welcomed him to the family.

Venetia smiled at him, the sort of smile he thought he would only ever see in a dream, one that seemed to outshine the sun itself.

"Tell me what you are thinking," she prompted.

Adrian brushed his fingertips over her lips. "I'm thinking that no man will ever be as blessed as I am to go from footman to husband—especially to *your* husband."

Venetia's eyes twinkled. "I think I am rather glad I sprained my ankle, or else we might never have met."

He burst out laughing, and she wrinkled her brow in confusion.

"What?" she asked.

"I believe your grandmother would have found a

way to bring us together, regardless. She's very clever."

"She is indeed." Venetia turned thoughtful eyes toward her grandmother. "*Very* clever."

Lady Latham gripped her cane and smiled back at them, as if she knew exactly what they were saying about her.

"But she couldn't possibly have guessed all that would happen," Venetia mused.

"She didn't need to. She only needed to do one thing," Adrian said.

"What's that?"

"To make sure that I would be tempted by you." He gazed at her kissable lips, uncaring of the guests nearby.

Venetia's eyes softened. "And were you?"

"Never was there a man in all of England so tempted."

Adrian leaned down and stole another kiss, one that would scandalize everyone present, but he didn't care.

ONE WEEK LATER

Venetia watched her husband enjoy his breakfast and peruse the newspaper in their new London townhouse. Gwen was out having tea with a few friends early in the morning and had left Venetia and her new husband alone. Venetia took advantage of the time to watch her husband unobserved. How she adored him... even as he was frowning slightly as he read, she'd learned he did that when he was focusing intently on something.

He was still getting used to the more relaxed life of a man who had married an heiress. It hadn't been easy at first when she'd told her friends of the marriage, but after meeting Adrian, they had all seen what made him so perfect. Murmurs of him marrying her for money quickly dissolved. On each of the last seven mornings, he woke well before dawn, thinking he had to get dressed and work, but each time she kissed him and pulled him back down into their bed. It would take time, teaching him to live a different life, but she would enjoy it.

He folded his paper and looked in her direction. "I thought I might adjust the hours of the staff, with your permission."

"Oh?" This piqued her curiosity.

"I thought of shortening their hours but not reducing wages. We can afford it." He proposed this carefully, respectful of the fact that the money he had access to came from Venetia's inheritance. He was keeping to his word and treating their marriage as a partnership.

"As you have the most knowledge of that field, I leave that decision to you."

Adrian relaxed and smiled at her, his expression peaceful. She'd never realized how tightly wound he had been until after they had married. He had become someone different, someone better—more relaxed and happier. Life in service had been hard, but now he had a chance to live more peacefully. It was only natural that he would wish to ease the load of the servants in his new home.

Their butler, Mr. Evanston, appeared in the doorway. "Sir, you have a visitor." He came to the table and held out a silver tray with a calling card on it.

"*I* have a visitor?" Adrian exchanged a puzzled glance with Venetia before he picked up the card. The butler waited patiently as Adrian read the card. He paled and handed the card to Venetia.

"The Duke of Stratford? Your father's here?" She reached across the table and touched his arm. "What do you wish to do?"

"I . . ." He shook his head. "I suppose it would be good to see him."

"Do you wish for me to accompany you?" Venetia watched Adrian with concern. The pallor on his face was disconcerting. He'd been careful not to speak much of his father, or the rejection that had burned Adrian so deeply early in his life.

"Please come," Adrian said without hesitation. "I will feel better if you are there."

They told Evanston to show the duke into their drawing room, and then they joined their unexpected guest. The duke was tall and thin, but strong. He was in his late fifties and in many ways was a mirror of his son, with amber eyes and dark hair now streaked with gray at the temples. When he saw Adrian, he stilled his pacing and squared his shoulders.

"Thank you for coming to visit us, Your Grace," Venetia began.

"Mrs. Montague," the duke greeted formally, and then his gaze moved back to Adrian.

"Would you care to sit?" Venetia suggested. "I could have some tea brought in."

Adrian and his father shared a long, silent look before the duke replied.

"If your husband has no objection, I would very much like that."

Adrian waved at the chairs in the room. "Please, sit."

The duke chose one and sat, and Venetia and Adrian took a pair of chairs facing him.

"I regret that this call comes so late," the duke said. "I was unsure if I would be welcome, but Lady Latham recently visited me and gave me her assurance that you would agree to see me."

"My grandmother visited you?" Venetia couldn't

help but wonder when her grandmother had done that. She had been spending more time out of the house now that Venetia was married. When Venetia had told her she didn't need to leave them alone so often, her grandmother had stroked her cheek fondly and smiled with a twinkle in her eye and had said, *"Trust me, my dear, you'll look back on these early days with the fondest smile and it's best that you have time alone with him before the babes arrive."*

The duke's expression transformed to one of amusement.

"She reminded me that I am not a coward. Yet these last ten years I have been behaving very cowardly. Both of my other children did without hesitation what I failed to do, which is to welcome you into my life, Adrian."

The duke swallowed hard. "I have made many mistakes—not marrying your mother, not keeping her at my home, not ever seeing you . . . not taking you in when you came to my door because I was too afraid to see you. Lord Devon did me a great service by hiring you, but I should have been the one to take care of you." The duke's gaze lowered to the floor. "I don't expect forgiveness for my mistakes, and I certainly do not deserve it."

"But you have it," Adrian said quietly.

The duke's brows rose, and he smiled. "In that case, I believe my belated wedding gift will be a welcome one." He removed a folded packet of papers from his coat pocket. "Please, accept this from me as my congratulations on your marriage."

He gave the papers to Adrian, who unfolded them. He scanned the contents and then passed the papers to Venetia without a word. Venetia read through the documents, and her mouth fell open.

"This is the deed to the Latham country estate," she whispered. "How . . . ?" She couldn't finish.

"Your grandmother told me how your cousin sold it for profit. She also told me that it was the house that you and she had called home and that you missed it most dearly. I had my solicitor approach the new owner and make an offer. It now belongs to you both."

Adrian rubbed his jaw as he stared at his father. "Thank you, Your Grace," he finally said. "This means a great deal to us."

"I hope to do much more, but I believe this is a good start," the duke replied. "If you won't object to me becoming a part of your lives."

Venetia could see that Adrian was still stunned by this visit, but she hoped he would view it positively.

"I would like that, Your Grace," Adrian said.

"Richard, please, and perhaps someday you will call me *Father*. When you feel comfortable with it."

Adrian held out his hand to the duke. "Richard."

"Let me get us some tea." Venetia rang the small bell for Evanston.

They spent the next half hour with Adrian's father, and when he departed, Venetia curled her arms around her husband's neck.

"How do you feel?" she asked him.

"Stunned," he said. "But hopeful."

"Hope is good."

She pulled his head down to hers for a kiss. She squealed in delight as he scooped her up and carried her back to one of their more comfortable settees in the drawing room. They both sat, Venetia on his lap, and continued kissing. Adrian's hand slid up her skirt, making her giggle as he tickled her with his fingertips. He always knew how to drive her mad with hunger for him.

"You meant to take me here?" Venetia pretended to ask in a scandalized gasp.

"Of course, we have only a few hours before your grandmother returns, and we mustn't waste a moment alone."

Venetia laughed. "You know she doesn't mind..."

"Well I mind. I adore your grandmother, but she's quite fierce. I always expect her to swoop in and knock me senseless with that cane."

"She would never!" Venetia laughed. "You are her hero, you know. You did exactly what she'd hoped, you gave Patrick a good thrashing."

Adrian's eyes burned with wicked delight as he gazed at her mouth again with a lusty fixation.

"You really do tempt me you know" he said, chuckling between their kisses.

"Do I now?" She bit his bottom lip playfully, and he groaned before kissing her harder.

"Minx," he growled, and Venetia laughed in delight.

"Hush and make love to me," she commanded.

Adrian flashed her a seductive look that made her body hum with excitement. "As you wish."

THANK YOU SO MUCH FOR READING TEMPTING THE Footman, the House of Devon Book 5! If you love my writing, don't miss out on more steamy timeless romances!

To know when my next book releases follow me here:

Book Bub

Newsletter

And join my VIP Reader Group on Facebook!!

Don't miss the next delightful romance in the House of Devon Series, Tempted by the Wallflower by Sue London.

The Duelist's Seduction
The Rakehell's Seduction
The Rogue's Seduction
The Gentleman's Seduction
Standalone Stories
Tempted by A Rogue
Bewitching the Earl
Boudreaux's Lady
No Rest for the Wicked
Devil at the Gates
Seducing an Heiress on a Train
Sins and Scandals
An Earl By Any Other Name
A Gentleman Never Surrenders
A Scottish Lord for Christmas

Contemporary
The Surrender Series
The Gilded Cuff
The Gilded Cage
The Gilded Chain
The Darkest Hour
Love in London
Forbidden
Seduction
Climax
Forever Be Mine

Paranormal

Dark Seductions Series

The Shadows of Stormclyffe Hall

The Love Bites Series

The Bite of Winter

His Little Vixen

Brotherhood of the Blood Moon Series

Blood Moon on the Rise (coming soon)

Brothers of Ash and Fire

Grigori: A Royal Dragon Romance

Mikhail: A Royal Dragon Romance

Rurik: A Royal Dragon Romance

Sci-Fi Romance

Cyborg Genesis Series

Across the Stars

The Krinar Eclipse

The Krinar Code by Lauren Smith writing as Emma Castle

Lauren SMITH
TIMELESS ROMANCE

Lauren Smith is an Oklahoma attorney by day, author by night who pens adventurous and edgy romance stories by the light of her smart phone flashlight app. She knew she was destined to be a romance writer when she attempted to re-write the entire *Titanic* movie just to save Jack from drowning. Connecting with readers by writing emotionally moving, realistic and sexy romances no matter what time period is her passion. She's won multiple awards in several romance subgenres including: New England Reader's Choice Awards,

Greater Detroit BookSeller's Best Awards, and a Semi-Finalist award for the Mary Wollstonecraft Shelley Award.

To Connect with Lauren, visit her at:
www.laurensmithbooks.com
lauren@laurensmithbooks.com

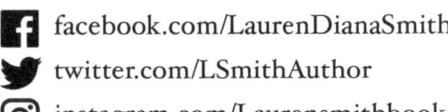

facebook.com/LaurenDianaSmith
twitter.com/LSmithAuthor
instagram.com/Laurensmithbooks